About the Author

Eunice Wormald worked for the BBC Open University and Care Home for people with Learning Difficulties. She retired to Norfolk in 2000 when she could no longer work due to osteo arthritis. She wrote *Lady in Waiting* in 2003 for a competition in Australia. At the age of 55 she suffered a brain stem stroke and is now paraplegic. She has 2 children whom she raised as a single parent.

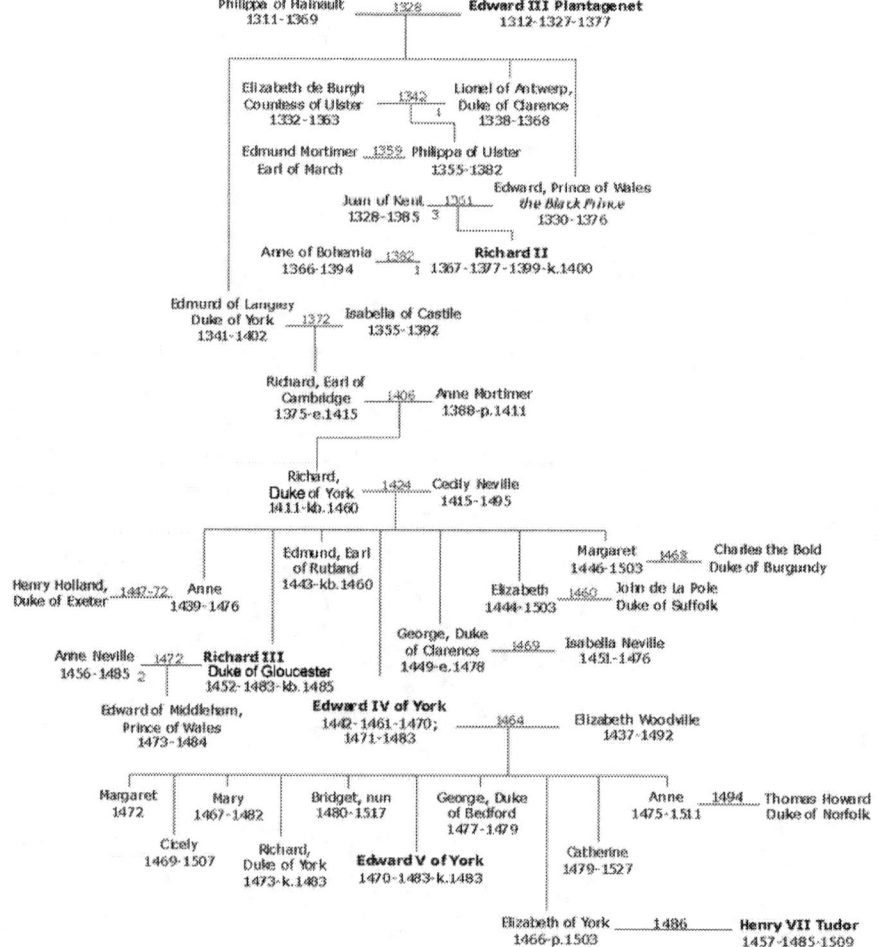

Philippa of Hainault 1328 Edward III Plantagenet
1311-1369   1312-1327-1377

Elizabeth de Burgh   1342   Lionel of Antwerp,
Countess of Ulster   Duke of Clarence
1332-1363   1338-1368

Edmund Mortimer 1359 Philippa of Ulster
Earl of March   1355-1382
                                    Edward, Prince of Wales
                   Juan of Kent   1361   the Black Prince
                   1328-1385   3   1330-1376

Anne of Bohemia 1382   Richard II
1366-1394   1   1367-1377-1399-k.1400

Edmund of Langley
Duke of York   1372   Isabella of Castile
1341-1402   1355-1392

Richard, Earl of
Cambridge   1406   Anne Mortimer
1375-e.1415   1368-p.1411

Richard,
Duke of York   1424   Cecily Neville
1411-kb.1460   1415-1495

                                   Margaret   1468   Charles the Bold
Edmund, Earl   1446-1503   Duke of Burgundy
of Rutland
1443-kb.1460   Elizabeth 1460 John de la Pole
                                   1444-1503   Duke of Suffolk
Henry Holland, 1447-72 Anne
Duke of Exeter   1439-1476
                                   George, Duke
                                   of Clarence 1469 Isabella Neville
Anne Neville 1472 Richard III   1449-e.1478   1451-1476
1456-1485 2 Duke of Gloucester
              1452-1483-kb.1485

Edward of Middleham, Edward IV of York
Prince of Wales   1442-1461-1470;   1464   Elizabeth Woodville
1473-1484   1471-1483   1437-1492

Margaret   Mary   Bridget, nun   George, Duke   Anne   1494 Thomas Howard
1472   1467-1482 1480-1517   of Bedford   1475-1511   Duke of Norfolk
                                       1477-1479
        Cicely   Richard,   Catherine
        1469-1507   Duke of York   Edward V of York   1479-1527
                    1473-k.1483   1470-1483-k.1483

                                   Elizabeth of York 1486 Henry VII Tudor
                                   1466-p.1503   1457-1485-1509

LADY IN WAITING

An historical novel about the life of Lady Anne Neville, Duchess of Gloucester. Later to be Queen of England.

11 June1456 - 16 March 1485

Eunice Clover Wormald

Published 2006 by arima publishing

www.arimapublishing.com

ISBN 1 84549 139 4
ISBN 978 1 84549 139 10

Cover image – Richard III & his wife Anne Neville – Victorian glass (possibly by William Burges) – Cardiff Castle, Glamorgan. Provided courtesy of The Richard III Society, London, UK.

Printed and bound in the United Kingdom

Typeset in Garamond 11/14

Swirl is an imprint of arima publishing.

arima publishing
ASK House, Northgate Avenue
Bury St Edmunds, Suffolk IP32 6BB
t: (+44) 01284 700321

www.arimapublishing.com

Drawings on pages 86 & 144 by Peter Womack.

Dedicated to my friends Geoffrey Richardson and Ron Broughton,
to my parents Sadie and Stan Wormald
and to my two children Lev and Emma.

Introduction

The Beginning and The End

He was my Lord and my love, yet I did not want to do it.

For the first time in 11 years of happy marriage I was afraid.

He was going to London to be Lord Protector, and I was to follow him and I did not want to. I had no wish to live or be anywhere but at Middleham.

He was my husband and I must obey but for the first time it was duty not love that drove me.

Things were changing for us both – the changes for Richard were great – but so were the changes for me. No one knew of my changes. No one thought to ask or show they cared. For the first time I could not confide my feelings to Richard, because they had no substance, I had no words to describe the dread which gripped inside my breast and hurt like a physical wound, so that I thought my heart would explode, or break, or both.

Of one thing I was certain; I would not take Edward. He would live without the Court and all its intrigues and hopefully when Edward V could rule without Richard, we could come back, come home, and be a family again.

Chapter 1

The Beginning

Where could we go? Where could I take him? Thirty years on and I am with the one man I always wanted in my life, and now, three weeks after he turned up out of the blue, we are spending our first real time, time as a couple, together.

Having decided to 'go for it' and see if a relationship really would work, I was then off to Ireland with my job, thus disposing of two weekends in one fell swoop. Now he was coming, now we had time to be together, and I lay in bed pondering, wondering where we could go, somewhere special, and somewhere memorable.

Bosworth. It came to me from somewhere deep inside. Bosworth, a place nearby, which I had always wanted to visit, but never had, surely this would make it a memorable weekend?

We got into the car; me directing, him driving, through to Sutton Cheyney village where we turned towards the battlefield and began the long sweeping descent to the entrance.

"Where are we going?" He had asked, and on seeing the signs for Bosworth, started to search his memory, the name seemed familiar. The hairs stood up on the back of his neck, he told me as we drove down Richard's Road to the battlefield entrance and up to the shields set either side of the road. We stopped. They were the shields of Norfolk and Northumberland. Then we continued up to the battlefield site and parking area.

With instincts only guiding us, we walked to the gate that led to Ambion Wood and Richard's well. It was inscribed, "What does this say?" he asked and I read it out, not realising, until I finished, that I had just translated an inscription that was written in Latin, "but I don't know any Latin!" I gasped. As we walked further we experienced people, confusion, noise, the clash of arms, the sound of arrows. Like snapshots he saw, and felt, impressions of the battle, which had begun on Ambion Hill and ended on Redemore plain with the death of the King.

We walked along the path through the wood and the flashbacks stopped and so did we, then slowly we returned to the well. It all started again, like memories, his not mine and suddenly I was crying and holding him. "I left you, you had all this to cope with on your own, and I left you. It was easier for me to die than to live with out our son – and so I died, and left you to face all this alone," Oh my God, I didn't realise, I'm sorry, I'm so sorry."

The End

I stood by the well and sobbed. "He had lost everything, my Lord, in a short space of time, his brother, his son, and his wife. He had stood above the plain – alone – wondering why he was there. How had this happened?" He did not want this – had never wanted any of this, and now he was alone, fighting for a crown he had never wanted and now could not pass on, and I? I had died and left him. He had been my life but I had lost my son and that loss had consumed me, it was easier to die, and dying I had taken away his last reason to live.

*   *   *   *   *

The words had come of their own volition, what did they mean? I did not know, neither of us did. All we knew was that Richard III had died in battle on Redemore Plain, known as the battle of Bosworth. That his wife, Anne had died prior to this. The how's and why's and wherefores of the matter we did not know but with the feeling coming through so strongly in the two of us I knew that we had to find out. We had to know if what we had experienced had any truth in history.

Chapter 2
Reminiscences

My first memories are of my nurse Antoinette, and my mother. My feelings of being safe and feeling warm and cosy in front of a huge fireplace with tree trunks burning fiercely providing light as well as heat.

I suppose mother was a great Lady but when she had married my father she had not been the heiress, her cousin Ann had been the one to inherit Warwick: but Ann died and mother was the only direct heir left of the great Beauchamps, Mortimers and Despensers. Suddenly, my mother was heiress to all their wealth and land and power and my father, was Warwick. An Earl with more wealth, lands and power than any Lord in England. He would laugh out loud as he told the story an hundred times, with Isabel seated on a stool at his feet, he would lift me off mother's knee and hold me up, his arms outstretched, laughing, and I knew I was safe, father always made me feel safe.

    *   *   *   *   *

We lay together and I felt safe again, a feeling I had lost years ago, through times of hardship and struggle the only person I trusted to look after me was myself. Suddenly we were together again and I felt a sense of rightness, of belonging together, I turned in the bed, I was falling, my hand reached up to hold on to the velvet bed - hangings to stop my fall. What velvet bed hangings? I did not have a bed with hangings, velvet or otherwise, round it. He smiled at me, held on to me, stopped me falling, I felt safe.

    *   *   *   *   *

As children we travelled to Calais, where my father was Captain, and later Lord of the seas, both titles unwillingly given by Margaret of Anjou under the guise of the King's command. We had met the King! I remember the awe and excitement and that grandmamma Alice had been with us; we had come to Guisnes on our way home from Calais. I did not know home, having been a baby when my father was made lord of Calais. Isobel remembered though, or said she did and so I was as excited at the thought of going home, as I was of meeting the King.

Besides, he did not look like a King, where were all his fine clothes I began to ask mother loudly, only to be hushed and told I must not speak, unless the King spoke to me. But the King looked awkward as if he knew nothing of children and we were soon excused whilst he and father sat in conference.

We came to London and my parents sent us to Middleham whilst they journeyed to Walsingham to say thanks at the shrine. I learned when I was older that there had been an ambush from which they narrowly escaped and that they had found Warwick Castle ransacked by my father's enemies.

Warwick Castle, which gave father his title, was his home when father was not at Court. Whilst repairs were put in motion my parents, therefore lived at The Herber and we came to join them at Christmas.

*   *   *   *   *

The Herber

The house was decked in wreaths of holly, and laurel, ivy and mistletoe. Greenery was strewn in long thick strands across doorways and inter-twinning balustrades and up the stairs. Candles shone brightly day and night and all our statuettes of Our Lady and Joseph and the baby Jesus were honoured with strands of gold and silver entwining them. My parents attended Court, and I wondered about the King. My father and his cousins had, I knew some powerful disagreements with him. It was why we had been in Calais, and why my father had been in Ireland so long, with his Uncle.

The King had seemed so gentle when we had met him at Guisnes. Mild and simply dressed, unlike the fine clothes of his courtiers, he had worn only his coronation ring for us to kiss, he was tall but very thin, I thought. "More like a monk," mama had said later, "poor Henry." But why she should pity the King I did not understand. My father was raising an army, this I knew and my cousin Edward as Earl of March had gone to Wales to raise troops.

Grandpapa Salisbury left us mid-December to go with Uncle Richard to Wakefield and cousin Edmund had gone with them. Why could we all not spend Christmas together? I wondered but Mama had just hugged me to her and whispered for me alone to hear, "too risky." Even aunt Cecily had not travelled with her husband but stayed at their palace of Baynards with my cousins Richard and George and Margaret. I was the youngest being only 3 years of age, though insisting loudly that I was 'nearly four'. Richard and George had done much travelling around the country, whilst I was in Calais with my parents and Isobel.

They had been at Fotheringhay when the strife between their Father and the King caused their mother to move them from estate to estate, from the time the hostilities between the Court party and the Yorkist's flared into their first battle, in 1455. Richard was 3 and George 7 when their lives at Fotheringhay were disrupted and their sister Margaret's with them, as Margaret of Anjou guided her gentle husband through the battles that were to ensue.

Aunt Cecily decided to uproot her daughter and two youngest boys and regularly moved them to her husband's and cousin's manors and castles, afraid not of the King, but of the Queen's intent.

So they had found themselves, suddenly at seven and eleven years of age in the wrong place at the wrong time. For aunt Cecily had met up with her husband at Wakefield taking her two sons with her, to see their father and brothers, Edward and Edmund. There was to be a great battle but fortune had not favoured York. Never again would my aunt and uncle trust the Lancastrian boast of not making war on women and children. I never knew what happened but both boys would wake in the night at times, shouting and sometimes screaming.

Now, several battles later, it seemed as if all of us would be caught up in the contention between the Queen and the mine uncle, the Duke of York. Hence my Uncle Richard and grandpapa Salisbury had led their troops away from London, to save the city from pillage and to maintain the good will of the citizens. With their own families also remaining in London where they would, they hoped, be safe.

Warwick Castle, now replenished and refurbished, was to welcome us for the New Year and my aunt and my cousins were to come with us. My father had insisted on it, and besides, Mamma told her practically, "It will give your servants the chance to freshen up Baynards for your return." So it was to Warwick that the news first came. "Thank God we were all together," Mamma said later, "for how would Cecily have born the news alone?" Grandpapa and uncle Richard were dead, but more shockingly, so too was Edmund. He had escaped and being wounded had made his way into the town with a loyal servant, only to be cruelly butchered by Lord Clifford on Wakefield bridge. The Lancastrian leader had impaled him on a sword, declaring that it was revenge for his own family's deaths in battle. "Ay, in battle," Papa said, "not butchered when they were wounded."

My aunt shut herself away to grieve, whilst father made plans to go to London to raise an army, when she emerged it was to tell him calmly that she and her boys would go to Baynards and would my father help her send her boys to Burgundy? My father at once agreed. He had his own ships and now that the Lancastrian leaders were seen to kill in cold -blood, none of the boys were safe. Richard and George would be sent to Burgundy and mama and Isobel and I to Middleham with grandmamma. Father was now Earl of Salisbury, which meant that as well as Warwick and Middleham, all of Grandpapa's estates were now father's too. He would gather his forces from all over England to avenge his father and uncle but especially his young cousin.

We could not imagine how Edward felt, father and brother both dead and worse humiliated by the forces of Margaret of Anjou. Not only taken prisoner and tortured but then executed and their heads struck off and impaled on pikes above the gates of York, with a paper crown put on my Uncle's head. Edward made his way from the Welsh Marches at speed.

As Edward moved to join my father his men had been attacked by Jasper Tudor. It was on this field that Edward sensed his destiny, as the sun rose it was reflected in the sky, looking like three suns together, Edward declared it was a sign that his father, grandfather and brother watched over them and that York would win the day. William Hastings had joined him with a body of Warwickshire men, and the day was indeed won.

My father, not so fortunate, had been beaten by the forces of Lancaster, yet he gathered his men and rode to meet Edward and they made for London.

Chapter 3
To Be a King

Edward IV

Richard and George were sent for, from Burgundy and Edward was King. Nine days had seen the York cause go from defeat to celebration. Aunt Cecily, determined that her two young sons would not fall foul of Margaret of Anjou's armies had, only nine days prior to this, allowed my father to help her make the arrangements for their departure to Burgundy.

The plan was not put into action until St. Alban's. This second battle that my father had at this place was a disaster for him and York. Messengers arrived post haste to my mother, now at The Herber and aunt Cecily back at Baynards and also to my father's ships; which now slipped their moorings at Greenwich and crept up the Thames at night.

We were all at Baynard's the night they left. Confusing the Lancastrians by our numbers, my aunt had called it. Reckoning that if there were other children about the fact that two were missing would not be noted, at least until those two were safely in Burgundy.

I remember mother holding Isobel and myself close, whispering how glad she was that we were girls and did not have to leave her. Margaret too stayed, it was not felt that Margaret of Anjou would be interested in the females of York, "it is only our sons she kills," my aunt reflected bitterly.

Now, only nine days later and Edward and my father had entered London and George Neville, Father's brother, had asked the question at Paul's Cross, 'Would the people have Edward, as their true King?'

Knowing that Margaret of Anjou's army was in Coventry, as well as their reputation for rape, pillage and murder flying before them, the Londoners did not hesitate. With loud shouts of "Ay, we'll have him." Caps thrown in the air and "the bonny lad" and "A Warwick, A York!" rending the air.

A few days later Edward was formerly offered the Crown at Paul's Cross and when he accepted he was accompanied to Westminster Hall. Sitting on the throne his father had thought to have, Edward declared his intent. Before he would be crowned, he would rid England of the Lancastrian scourge. They had brought men from the North down to raze crops, burn and pillage homes and defile the women. Margaret of Anjou and her Scots would be drummed out of England. Then, and only then, would the coronation date be decided on.

We had never got to Middleham, and now London was safe we stayed, waiting for our cousin's return from Burgundy and our new King's victory. For we never doubted that Edward would be victorious.

My father left at once, to raise troops in the Midlands and five days later Edward too left London, secured by Yorkist and Warwick's troops, to join my father.

He had briefly come to see my Aunt, his mother, to tell her to bring her youngest sons home. He was tender with her but "We will be avenged, Mother, that," he said, "I promise." We were all sat in the Solar. Isobel struggling with her embroidery and I, who had been playing with the puppies, stopped to watch the scene. As children they ignored us, not seeking to be more private, not thinking that we understood. But I saw the emotion on Edward's face and his mother's and I quaked inwardly at the thought of ever being the source of Edward's displeasure. As he left he came over briefly and laid a hand on our heads, in turn, kissed my mother lightly and was gone.

All we would get now were messengers and reports but Richard and George were coming home and I smiled up at him, as he touched my head, a smile he answered with his own.

Edward had built up strong links with his two younger brothers. When all of them were in London, Edward had visited them everyday at John Paston's London home. I think he must have enjoyed Richard's adulation and George's precociousness. No one else could stand out in the shadow of Edward's brightness. Richard was most like his father but Edward was Richard's star. He loved Edward and from this time, I think, gave him his heart and soul.

So we waited and the news came. On March 29 the battle of Towton was fought, a snow blizzard obliterating everything and blowing into the Lancastrians faces. It became known as 'York's weather' whenever a fall of snow occurred, for somehow Edward and father won the day. Edward then made for York. The City council who opened the gates had forgotten whose heads would greet their new King, but he had not. Face white, lips thin, he had looked once and swept into the City with the words, "Remove them," thrown at my father, who reverently took the heads of his Cousin and father to have them interred with their remains. Later Edward had, in private, embraced him, apologising for not remembering that Papa's own father's head was above the gates too.

They called him The Kingmaker, my father, but in reality, at first anyway, before the power became all-important, he but followed in his father's footsteps.

Supporting his nephew, Edward Earl of March after the Duke of York's defeat, foul murder as it was called by many, at Wakefield.

When Edward was first King he gave his brothers titles that they were too young to appreciate, too young also to administer the power that went with such titles, he made them both Dukes, however, as befitted the brothers of a King.

Richard and George now lived at Baynards. Edward preferred the royal apartments at The Tower Palace and visited as often as he could, at Baynards. He watched his brother George, almost a man; who had had no training in arms, or of education since he had left Fotheringhay. No household had been safe for the son of York, so the Duke had not put George with a household to be educated and trained.

This should not happen to Richard. When we went to London for Edward's coronation and Richard and George were made Dukes, Edward asked my father to take his younger brother in hand, to educate and teach him courtly ways, how to be a knight and to fight for his King and country. There was none, Edward declared whom he could trust to imbue all this with faith and loyalty, only his Uncle Warwick. Edward did not command, he asked and my father took the compliment and my cousin. The next time he rode into the gates of Middleham, Richard rode with him.

So now that Edward was King my father and mother would educate Richard in the ways of letters, culture, musike and reading, and the ways of knighthood and warfare. As was the way for all young men of good families.

Edward chose Warwick, to give Richard the stability, often lacking in his young life and the education he would need, to help Edward keep his throne secure.

Chapter 4
Consanguinity

Isabel and I were cousins, to George and Richard. I being youngest of all, nevertheless we dealt very well together, when George visited, which seemed to be often, my good mother felt that, at last, she had two boys to bring up, that the good lord had denied her, for her self.

Richard was knighted by his brother Edward, when he was thirteen years of age. He was smaller than his brothers were and more slightly built. Richard was like his father, whereas Edward and George had the Plantagenet lusty build and fair/reddish hair.

Richard had a look of frailty and many wondered that he had survived thus far. Like his father he had courage and strength belied by his appearance. Edward loved his youngest brother and valued the devotion to him that shone in Richard's eyes anytime Edward was talked of, or, great joy, when Edward sent for Richard to join him.

So Richard came to our Castle at Middleham, up in the Dales, near the Yorkshire moors, a place well loved by the Neville family. It was home to all of them, my father and all his brothers and sisters alike. Nowhere was quite like Middleham.

This was to be no extended visit but home, a secure and stable environment for all the young knights in my father's care until they learned their trade. My father was no jouster, fighting was to kill or be killed not a pageant or tournament to entertain. So the young knights where trained, including Richard. Smaller than his brothers he may be, yet he had a strength other men envied. Taught to pull a longbow: one needed strength for that; and the archers trained them to build their muscles and expand their chests and to hold the bow straight and still on one drawn in breath to release death, silent, deadly and accurate.

In such a wise were they taught to fight with sword and dagger, mace and axe, chain and lance, spear and shield and how to balance on the ground as they did on a horse, lightly and evenly to distribute their weight. I think the hardest lesson must have been to learn to fight in full armour and I remember them in the court, sweat pouring from them, with the weight of the armour and the heat of the sun, but learn it they must, all of them.

Yet, because we were family and because Richard was the King's brother my own mother was as a mother to him, so that the bonds so forged, held. He came to us, in the quiet of a Sunday afternoon, after prayers had been said and dinner eaten. To sit in the Solar and chat pleasantly, to walk or ride with us to the Dales and to continue to learn, as we also did, from my mother, the art of management and respect for God.

*　　　　*　　　　*　　　　*　　　　*

Middleham

My goodness! It was beautiful. The April sunlight on the Castle walls making it warm and alive, the purple flowers overhanging the walls from nooks and crevices adding to the scene, with the green grass beneath and the hills beyond.

The new oak stairway was on the outside, where a stone staircase had been. A wooden platform stood above the great hall, which had once been a gallery leading to the solar and chapel their bedroom and Richard's 'office' where he had dealt with the daily business which included the running of Middleham, and giving the tenants their right to law.

We stood on the battlements and looked across the Courtyard to the Princes Tower, "How do you feel?" he asked me. I smiled, and took a photo of him leaning against the wall, and we made our way down the oak stairway across to the Princes Tower, Edward's tower.

*　　　　*　　　　*　　　　*　　　　*

I chose the tower for its privacy and the view over the moors. Up on the hill beyond were the ruins of the first Castle built at Middleham, but that had been mainly for defence and not big enough for the rapidly expanding Neville brood and their relations. So another, more modern, warmer castle was built. The heat from the huge kitchen fires made its way, along with the smoke, up the vast chimneys, which extended from floor to floor, and out through the roof, but every floor had a fire and vast chimneys and these served to heat the living quarters of the family. It could be cold in the Dales, even in summer the days could turn bitterly cold, and also the nights.

So the tower, Edward's tower, was built above a warm underground kitchen. The kitchen fires being kept burning to keep the Tower warm, as well as for use, if the Castle was busy with visitors. It became a sanctuary away from the hustle and bustle and the noise, not just for Edward and later his companions, but for us too.

*   *   *   *   *

We stood at the doorway of the Princes Tower, damp, crumbling, now a sanctuary for pigeons and sparrows, open to the sky. It was damp and cold, an empty shell, I turned and moved away, barely seeing, towards the wall of the Keep's Great Hall, it was warmer, sunny, a figure watching, I spoke involuntarily, "My Lord?"

Suddenly he was there again, urging me on to view the rest of the ruins of Middleham.

I don't know when liking, caring, friendship, became love. I was 10 years of age when Richard, now 13 and fully trained in all the accomplishments of knighthood was called back to Court. Not just to visit, but to take up his duties and his place at his brother's right hand, curious for one so young and, as yet, untried in battle. Though his wandering life, and my mother's good training, was grounding enough to point him on the right road, beside his beloved Edward. George was the more like to Edward in looks and stature, but Richard was more like him in logic and steadfastness. Hence he took the motto 'Loyaltie my Lie', loyalty binds me, and the white boar for York as well as the white rose, both established symbols of the house of York and Gloucester.

I remember him once, on a visit to see us. We were out hawking on the moors, just the two of us, and Richard plucked a piece of broom from a hillock, split it in two and placed a sprig in his bonnet pin and solemnly gave the other half to me. "My lady," he bowed "welcome to the house of planta genista." We laughed gaily at first, then wholly serious and I was in his arms and being kissed. He was 15 years old, I was 12 years of age, and much was to happen to both of us before we were to meet again.

Chapter 5
Returning

I was here, at last Middleham. We had decided on a holiday visiting the castles of Richard III in the North. Not 'his Castles' as such really, his homes, the places he and his wife and later his son also, called home. Sherriff Hutton was also on our itinerary but this was Middleham.

It was late in the day when we arrived but the Custodian said it would be fine for us to look round. "Where are you staying?" she asked. Our reply was that we did not know. We were in Middleham, and coming to see the castle was priority. Somewhere to stay was secondary to this; we'd sleep in the car if we had to. "There's a room at Domus." She told us; "just over the other side of the market square; but you'd need to go now to be sure of it."

We had an hour before closing, to look round the Castle; we were not going to waste it finding accommodation. This we explained to her, being here, in Middleham Castle was too important for us to worry about having somewhere to stay.

I was at Middleham! A feeling of joy and happiness welled up inside me. I raced from ruined room, to ruined room, imagining how it must have been. Suddenly I found my self heading towards a tower, "I'm back," where the words in my head, and then, "Margaret, I must tell Margaret." I stopped at the tower base crumbled into ruins. All was destroyed and Margaret, whoever she had been, was no more.

*　　　　*　　　　*　　　　*　　　　*

The north, was Percy and Neville territory, split between them and where my father could defend his own against great odds, if need be. I look back and see my father, not as others saw him, not as the great Earl of Warwick challenging Kings but as the more familiar, larger than life father around whom the household pivoted. His comrades in arms saw the soldier and the statesman but to his family he was a father and husband.

Our first sight of Middleham I do remember, it was Easter, and fortunately a particularly warm one; for I knew that the north could also be cold and forbidding. A purple flower flourished in the surrounding countryside and high on a knoll, but within walking distance, was the first Neville Castle at Middleham built before the present one, our Middleham.

*   *   *   *   *

I'm not sure of my feelings on being taken from Calais to meet the King in England. I remember crowds of people and banners and flowers and thinking that Papa must be so good and clever to be so loved by everyone, and so grand. My parents sent us on to Middleham. Whilst they progressed around their estates, going to Walsingham, so my mother told us later to give thanks for their lives, after surviving an ambush of Lancastrian soldiers. At Middleham the local villagers all turned out to bid us welcome and to catch a glimpse of the two Neville daughters, whom they had never seen. They waved and cheered and Isabel and I waved back, glad of the welcome, which helped us to feel that we where indeed coming home.

Antoinette and the main household servants had come on ahead some weeks ago, to ensure that all was as my lady mother required. No task mistress, her gentle words were law and not solely due to her husbands ever present aura but also due to her own ability, learnt as a girl from her own mother, to be firm but fair. I don't know what she would have been like if anyone had stepped out of line, for no one ever did, from the meanest scullion to the castle steward my mother earned respect and obedience. Her job, as it would one day be Isabel's and mine, was to ensure good stewardship of her Lord's estates. Estates brought to her Lord not by dowry but due to her cousin's death, which left her as heir to the Beauchamp, Mortimer and Dispenser lands and fortune; hence she became Countess of Warwick and my father the Earl.

*   *   *   *   *

How was Middleham for me in those early days? An adventure, at first, a little bit frightening because all was new to us. It was not as big as our castle at Calais, which we knew from kitchen to turret and so we felt, Isabel and I, that we would soon get to know this new home as well.

I remember when we discovered the stairway from the great hall up onto the battlements. A great adventure at the time, we had slipped away to play in the castle garden, a small enclosed kitchen garden, with sweet herbs growing, and roses, my mother loved roses and trees covered in white blossom in the spring, all had been planted under her direction. The stairway was off to the right and joined the main outer stone stairway, but this way was narrow and dark and infinitely more exciting to two young girls, barely able to climb in our long skirts, which were totally unsuitable for clambering anywhere. Although I recall, that never stopped us. So we played, imagining ghosts peering out of the stairways dark curves. Then we were out on the gallery that surrounded the hall, and led to all sorts of rooms including the Solar and a chapel. My favourite thing was to turn the other way out onto the stone stairway, through a heavy wooden door and to follow the steps round and out on to the battlements.

The wind caught our hair and our clothing and we would pull off our caps to let our hair free to play with the wind. The view, on a sunny day, looked over the Castle Court and fields and the original castle which, gradually falling into ruin, still stood impressive against a blue sky with sunlight bathing the stone walls in a warm glow. When it was cold and blustery the old castle seemed to be gripping onto the hill on which it stood, as if daring the weather to do its worst, its' outline dark against the scudding darkening clouds.

I would creep away from even Isabel at times, when I wanted my thoughts to fly free and to stand there, on 'my battlements', and if a lookout was posted, to watch for a messenger from my father. Then, someone would lift me up to see from their eye level, and I would look towards the main gate through which messengers would come pounding.

"Excuse me," we turned, and the Custodian was coming towards us, "I hope you don't mind but I've booked it for you." We walked towards her, enquiringly, "the room, at Domus," she explained, "I knew you would not get anywhere tonight, so I booked it. It's a lovely house and just across the square. I hope you don't mind." She repeated. Mind, of course we did not mind, we thanked her for her consideration, we would go over straight away as the Castle was closing. "You know," she said, "as you have paid full price for your tickets, and only had an hour, you may use them tomorrow if you want to visit again." Of course we would want to visit again, we thanked her and made our way to the Hotel.

As promised Domus was both warm and friendly and we settled in, and then got ready to go out in the evening for a meal. The town, now with modern links to horseracing, still has the medieval paving; its houses built mainly from castle stone. For me the sense of history was all around us. We decided on the pub just across the Market Square and there was a lovely log fire burning in the grate.

I sat on the settle, near to the fire and facing the bar. People turned to stare at us, I wondered if I was in the seat used and saved for a local person, but no one moved me, and I waited as he went to the bar to order our drinks and get menus. He seemed to be taking a long time and I went to enquire if we had to order our meals at the bar. No, I was told they would come and get our orders and bring our drinks, I was to sit down and not worry all would be done.

Sure enough our drinks arrived and our order was given, and soon a lovely meal was in front of us. It was warm, comfortable and familiar and more drinks were brought to us. As we relaxed I watched the other diners. They were not being waited on, I noticed but had to order at the bar and get their own drinks, what was going on, or was I imagining it? When I had approached the bar the woman serving had fallen over herself to assure me of her attention, and that I had no need to exert myself, "she almost curtsied" I had muttered to him, perhaps a trifle ungratefully.

Later we returned to Domus and sat with another couple and our host in the lounge. After our host left the other couple turned to us, "Who are you?" the chap asked, we wondered what he meant, "well," he said "we noticed you in the pub. They were waiting on you hand and foot and we wondered why, none of us were waited on, so we thought you must be important." So we had not imagined it. Who were we? What had been going on? Was it a time slip? We would definitely visit the castle the next day.

The sky was dark, a yellow tinge had presaged the snow that had fallen all day and a thick blanket enveloped the hills.

*   *   *   *   *

The King was in London for New Year and father and George were to accompany Richard to London as soon as Christmas was done. All summoned by Edward to try and reconcile my father to his 'protégés' wooing of a Burgundian alliance.

Father felt that Edward had, once again, made him the fool, on the political stage. For he had been pursuing diplomacy with Louis whilst Edward wooed Burgundy.

He had wrote to father, calling him his 'good friend'. Father had read the letter aloud in the solar, scoffing at this seeming attempt at reconciliation. "How would this help?" father stormed, Edward was still married to the Wydville witch!

This time, he vowed, he would not forgive Edward lightly.

I saw Richard flinch, his loyalties torn between my father, whom he loved right well and his brother Edward, the King. George threw a log on the fire, "First," he said, "let us put all behind us and enjoy our Christmas revels. A fine feast, with musike and mummers." He bowed to my mother, acknowledging her organisation of this. "We will have a fine time," he declared, "and you will dance with me, Isobel?" he asked my sister. Who blushed suddenly and said that she would and that right gladly. I wondered why Isobel should blush to be asked to dance with George. They had danced together often enough, but I was still a child, being only ten years, where Isobel was almost a woman grown and, though I did not realize it, looking to George for a husband.

My uncle, George, was back in favour after refusing to attend the celebrations for the diplomatic mission from Burgundy, cut short by the Duke's death. Now Charles was Duke, Richard had told me, and his sister like to be Duchess of Burgundy, if the negotiations went well. Edward wanted to balance the power of France with Burgundy as ally. Edward, never one to hold a grudge soon had my uncle, now Archbishop of York, back in his favour.

"Edward does not want to replace us," he told my father, "only to balance our power with the Wydvilles. Just as he is trying to do with Burgundy and France, wishing to keep them both as allies."

I turned my back on the chat of politics. The blazing fire and the room, decked with holly and mistletoe. The holly had a mass of red berries, sign of a harsh winter the servants said. I knelt on a seat and looked out across the Castle to the snow bound hills, 'twould be quiet, with Richard and George gone.

*   *   *   *   *

We had never visited Middleham in the winter before. Snow lay everywhere and I wanted photo's of the Castle. The silence was eerie and the great hall looked stark and dark against the whiteness of the snow.

"That will make a lovely photo." I breathed out and a white mist of cold accompanied my words.

*   *   *   *   *

The castle was quiet and Isobel and I sat embroidering a large tapestry between us. It was a hunting scene and I fidgeted, wanting to be out with my horse and dogs. Mother had deemed it too cold for us to join the hunting party and so we were sat, embroidering a scene of horses, flowers and trees.

"First the Widow Grey," my mother tutted over her piece of the tapestry, "and now ignoring France for Burgundy. Keeping your father in the dark, in truth Edward may be King but who has put him there?" Isobel glanced at me and smiled and I remembered Richard's account of his first meeting with the Queen.

It had been a great scandal and Edward wanted Richard to approve his choice and to like his Queen. Instead they had cordially disliked one another on sight. Richard had not seen her outward beauty and had looked straight into her eyes and seen her cold and calculating heart. Elizabeth had been expecting another, smaller version of Edward and George; Richard being only 12 years of age; instead she saw a dark haired, serious boy, who had looked straight into her eyes and soul ,before lowering his, not out of respect but because Richard kept his thoughts to himself.

He had behaved impeccably, as he had been taught, by my mother and his own but also by his experience of life, which had been hard for one so young. The Queen had accepted his homage and declared how unlike the rest of the House of York Richard was. Edward had chewed his nether lip and replied, tersely, that "Richard was much like his father." "Not a good beginning" Richard had said to me, laughing and then declared that, as he had no interest in court politics and preferred the north, they did not have to meet too often.

*   *   *   *   *

Middleham, again, I heaved a sigh of content as we walked into the castle's shop. Maureen, the custodian, was there and we chatted, with him telling her that I was buying 'Yet more books!' I knew what I was looking for; there was a new book out by the author Geoffrey Richardson. I had read The Lordly Ones, and had, in fact brought it with me, now a new book had been written and I wanted it, along with anything else that I did not have about the period known as The Wars of the Roses. Someone came into the shop as I found the books I wanted and I heard Maureen behind me, greeting them. Then I caught her words, "well it's not often we get a famous author in the shop," and the reply, "Famous? You know I'm not famous." I turned and saw a slightly built man, quite tall, in a dark grey suit. I held the books I wanted and asked, "Famous author? Why who are you?" The man did not answer, only looked a trifle embarrassed. 'A nobody' I thought, 'just a friend of Maureen's.'

"Don't you know who this is?" Maureen asked me. "You wanted his book." I started forward as she carried on speaking, "this is Geoffrey Richardson," she said. "You?" I asked, incredulous, "you're Geoffrey Richardson?"

"Yes." Came the reply. I ran down the shop and flung my arms round him, "I've got your books," I gasped, all of them, "I think they're wonderful - you are a wonderful, wonderful man."

*　　　　*　　　　*　　　　*　　　　*

"Sit still Anne," my mother smiled at me struggling with the embroidery. "You're stabbing at that piece, you're not actually hunting, you know, only depicting a hunt." I wanted to be out, riding my horse and exercising my dogs. They weren't really all my dogs of course; they belonged to father, to the castle, to help with the hunt. They were not to be petted or spoiled my father had warned me. Yet I could not help getting attached to some of them. Especially when the bitches whelped and we had puppies everywhere. Isobel and I had insisted on naming them all and it was these young dogs and bitches that joined our excursions on to the moors. Here we could gallop our horses and the young dogs learnt to follow us and were kept in check by the boys who helped to train them to join the pack.

This is what I allowed my mind to wander over as I stitched the tapestry, watching the embroidered dogs leap through embroidered trees and fields of flowers.

There was a clatter of hooves on the drawbridge and before mother could speak, Isobel and I had dropped our side of the tapestry as Antoinette came, quietly, in the room. "'Tis my lord, my lady." Was all we heard and we were out of the Solar and across the Great Hall to the steps, still slippery with snow.

Pattens awaited by the door and we thrust our slippered feet into them, as we demanded a servant open the latch of the huge outer door, so that we could scamper down the great stone stairway and into our father's arms.

Laughing and chiding us, because it was too cold for us to be out, especially without warm woollen cloaks, he opened his own huge fur cloak and enveloping us both, half lifted us, still laughing, back up the stairs and into the postern gate.

*　　　　*　　　　*　　　　*　　　　*

Reconciliation

Attending court functions was part of my mother's life. Usually, we went with her, staying at Baynards castle with Richard's mother, my aunt Cecily, so that, away from the hustle and bustle of court life we could have some semblance of normality. The Herber was our family home but so full of noisy retainers and the great lords seeking favours of my father, that my mother and aunt had agreed to use Baynards as a retreat for them and us.

The court had learnt quickly that both Edward and his mother frowned upon any who tried to gain favour with him through his beloved mother. My Aunt was proud of her son but she did not seek to influence him. So the petitioners sought my father's approval and The Herber was a continuous throng of people. The kitchens were kept open, at my father's orders, and each person coming to his gate could take enough meat as he could carry on his dagger. So the people of London loved him, none would starve whilst Warwick was in town and the cry went up whenever he was out, "A Warwick, A Warwick" and men gave their loyalty to the ragged staff.

My aunt was called 'proud Cis', by those who could not gain access to her son through herself. To her family and to us, her nieces, she was 'aunt,' kind and thoughtful, warm and loving, not sentimental or silly but with a wisdom gained from following my Uncle Richard on his travels and having to make a home wherever the King sent them.

Just as we had lived in Calais, with father, so aunt Cecily had made homes in France and in Ireland, her children going with her, many of them born out of England, Edward in Rouen and George in Ireland, Richard was the only surviving son who had been born here in England.

Whilst my father waited at The Herber for his and my cousin George's summons, Richard was at Westminster Palace preparing for Edward's entry into London.

The King would enter the city via Cheapside, the better for the ordinary people to see him. House after house hung garlands and flags with the King's device - the Sunne in Splendour, as well as the devices of York, the Falcon and Fetterlock and the White Rose.

George joined Richard at Westminster and they rode to meet their brother together with a following of Nobles and Ladies, including my aunt and my mother and waited at the city gates. The Lord Mayor and 22 Alderman in scarlet robes, with 200 guilds represented in the deep blue of the House of York.

"The cheers were deafening," Richard told us later, "and Edward rode through the streets followed by the Mayor and his people. Then we met up with him, George and I." He grinned broadly at the memory. "Edward stopped his horse and waited for us. We dismounted and walked towards him and knelt one either side of his horse, there in the snow, Oh how the crowd cheered at that and he raised us both up and called us his dear and most beloved brothers. Then Harre and John pushed past William Hastings and Edward's senior lords, in their excitement. I thought Edward would chide them but he just smiled and extended his hand for them to kiss. They all but fell to the ground in their hurry to dismount. Then Edward called for Warwick, loud and clear and the horses and the crowd parted and mine Uncle rode slowly through the parted company, his hat off and his arm extended as he bowed low in the saddle. Edward called him 'dear coz' and 'best friend' and so they rode through the streets side by side, with the crowd cheering and throwing up their caps, just as they used." He paused then, "but I think me the Queen did not like to see their amity, ay and so George said too."

He finished and George nodded, "Ay Dickon be right there, methinks the Wydville's are no friends to us nor the Nevilles. She does not like that Richard and I be so close to our Uncle and cousins." He smiled and he and Isobel exchanged a fleeting glance.

Chapter 6
Planta Genista

I clutched the sprig of bloom tightly in my hand as if it would disappear if I loosed my grip. As I walked through the Great Hall my mother came up to meet me, looking concerned, "Anne, Anne, where have you been? Look at you, your face is smudged and, why! What is that you carry in your hands?"

"It is, it is, Mama" my voiced trembled sure I was going to be robbed of my treasure; I held it up for my mother to see. "Planta genista," my father's voice came suddenly, and there he was, beside my mother, smiling. "Yes Papa, I agreed. "And who gave you this?" he queried. "Why," I replied, "it was, it was, Richard" my voice had gone quieter, remembering our embrace and sudden kiss, had I done wrong?

"Richard indeed," my father boomed, "well, well, a most fortunate flower my lass, and a promising sign, and what did Richard say my lass?" father was looking at me intently, but a half smile still hovered around his mouth.

* * * * *

"He, he said it made me part of his house, planta genista being from whence the Plantagenet name comes, you know Papa." I was coaxing, wheedling, not wishing the flowering sprig to be taken from me.

"And you like that, Anne?" father asked me, "being part of Richard's house?" I nodded, hardly daring to breath, leave alone speak. At that the atmosphere lightened as my father lifted me up, easily he was so strong, to his eye level and kissed me on the mouth. My mother watched, a smile on her face too, I was relieved, had expected anger, but instead my parents seemed pleased, even proud of me. As my father set me down our maid, one-time nurse came down the stairs from the Solar and as we all turned, my father set me down gently, on to my feet. "Antoinette," my mother spoke, "please take Lady Anne to her chamber."

"Ay," my father interrupted, "see she gets a warm bath in pleasant herbs and flowers, she has had a busy day."

He took my mother's hand in his, as Antoinette gave a slight curtsy of acknowledgement, and led me out of the hall, up the stairs, and across to my bedchamber.

*   *   *   *   *

Chapter 7
Barnard Castle

I caught a glimpse of the bird, high and to my left, and brought my arm up instinctively as a perch. Too high, she would try again, so I had time to brace myself for her weight, and swung my right arm into the correct position for her to land safely.

*　　　　*　　　　*　　　　*　　　　*

As I swung round, arm up, the sunlight brought me up short, what was I doing? Standing in what had been an inner moat, below the Castle at Barnard in Yorkshire, now County Durham, with my right arm held out as a perch. I shook my head to bring myself back to the present.

It had upset me, that there was no information about the Nevilles, on the tape we listened to, as we walked round the castle, Richard III was also barely mentioned. I felt too, that had the signs of the Boar not been found above a grand window, and elsewhere, his residence at 'Barny' would have been totally overlooked. The castle, in the warm sun felt warm and friendly and familiar.

This was a Neville castle, like Richmond and Raby, yet first Richmond and now Barnard Castle gave no history, which told of either the Neville's influence, or Richard's, who had done so much for the North, and who had been Earl of Richmond.

Why were the northerners so loathe to associate with his name? Whereas the Midlands, where I had lived for over 15 years, looked on him as their 'Good King,' and are proud of their association with him.

*　　　　*　　　　*　　　　*　　　　*

Chapter 8
Sherriff Hutton

We looked round the ruins of what was once a manorial castle, with gardens and moat, or water feature, a castle which was now a cluster of mute, stark, pointers of dark brick and stone stretching like fingers, into a clear blue sky. With most of the castle in ruins, or sunk into the mound on which it was built, some of its buildings housing farm equipment. Little remained to remind one of its time as a Neville Manor and later as the seat of the Council of the North, formed by the north's 'good lord' Richard Plantagenet, Duke of Gloucester.

As we left the castle, a local man pointed us in the right direction for the church. "Ay, it's down there, it's where the Prince of Wales is buried, or so they say."

We approached St. Helen's, as dusk crept in, and entered the church. Part of it was renovated, but where was the tomb of the Prince? I had expected to 'feel' something, as I had at Nottingham, a pull, a feeling of grief, something to lead me to the tomb, but I 'felt' nothing. I returned to the door of the church and saw the postcards of Edward's tomb but where was it? I had looked in the Neville Chapel and it was not there. I walked to the front of the church and looked left instead of right. It was there, a boy's figure, in a long gown, in effigy on the top. Repaired after being "found in a ruinous state" out in the churchyard. 'Once thought to have been in the Neville Chapel,' I read.

The tiles where cold on my knees as I knelt down next to the catafalque. I looked at the designs on the tomb, and compared them with the copy of the manuscript on the window ledge above it, which showed the designs commissioned by Richard, for his son's tomb. All seemed to say that this was their boy. So why did I 'feel' nothing? As I stood looking at the catafalque, I tried to imagine, to feel, how the parents must have felt to lose a child, even in the high risk days of infant mortality, especially a child who had survived the early years, what a blow, heart-rending. I left the church, and found him looking round the churchyard, it was evening and clouding over, time to leave. We stood at the car and looked back towards the church, the clouds gathering, then, as we were about to get into the car the sun broke through and lit up the church, bathing it in sunlight, like the arm of heaven giving it an angelic light. The moment was symbolic, to us and we were filled with awe. I knew we would return.

Chapter 9
London

"Right, how do you want it?" My hairdresser sprayed my dry hair to dampen it. I never went in for the 'full works'. Shampooing or blow-drying, I was too impatient. "The same style please, I replied, "only short, very short, I get so hot and my hair seems to grow so quickly."

"Over your ears or behind?"

"Oh, behind please, so my earrings can be seen, when I wear them."

I have, also, never been one for small talk at a hairdresser, the stylists and clients seemed to know all the intimate details of one another's lives. I was half-envious of the chatter but knowing deep inside that it was not for me. I'd managed some sort of 'small talk' with other Mums when the children were young, but it was not really me. You're a snob; I told myself reprovingly and shook my head at my reflection in the mirror.

∗   ∗   ∗   ∗   ∗

I awoke, cold and shivering on a damp horsehair mattress, which smelt stuffy and un-aired. The room was dark; there was a window, of sorts, stretched animal skin over the opening, letting in a limited sort of yellowish light. Where was I? A shiver shook my whole body, from the very top of my head, through to my very toes and fingertips. My head ached and I felt woozy. A nightmare! That was it! I was having a nightmare! I must wake myself up. Richard would laugh at me when I next got to see him. Whenever that might be, I reflected ruefully. Cousin George had so many excuses for us not to meet. I wondered how long it would be before Richard's tolerance and good humour gave way. He was, after all, a tried and tested battle Commander. Whereas George, I shrugged to myself, George was a traitor. Words I dare only think but never voice. For no matter what heinous offence he committed, George always seemed to come out of it, "Smelling of roses." Someone said once. "Yes," I thought, "White roses, the white rose of York and his brother, the King." I began to wonder how long Ned would tolerate George's insolence, when I sat up with a start. Wool gathering. Wool gathering! What had happened to the nightmare?

I opened my eyes wide, pinched my arms and tried to stand, this was no nightmare, this was real! I could feel the fear and the screams, rising in my throat.

"Oh, yer awake, are yer?" A door opened, letting in hardly anymore light, and a large, comfortable looking woman stood in the doorway, gazing down at me. Not unfriendly, I gauged but not to be trifled with either. "Where, where am I?" I tried to sound strong and in control, but my voice came out in a whisper and my fear, I was sure, was palpable. "Why dearie," was the response, "no need to take on so. Jack's got you out that awful place and now you be home."

"Awful place?"

"Ay dearie, you bain't be good at remembering, I daresay, but we'll try and give you a good home. Long as you don't become loud or violent o'course but o'course you won't, you don't wanta go back to the mad house, me lady. No. You just be'ave like a good lass and me an' my Jack, well' now we're set up, we can afford to look after ya, so we can. When Jack asked me about ya, I says 'o'course,' I says, bring the lass 'ere. You being kindred like, and not given to doing anyone harm. So I hear. Just got some strange ways, haven't you? Sort of 'airs and graces' like? Well, that won't do any harm to this lot as works 'ere. P'raps a bit of good manners 'll likely rub off on 'em." She paused for breath and then finished. "Only you munna ask 'em to call you yer ladyship, or anything, 'cos they might take that funny. Agreed girlie?" I gazed at her, wide-eyed, unable to respond.

"That's right. We'll soon get you cleaned up and out o' them old rags. Find you some'ent decent to wear. Tho' you be mighty thin. Still we'll see what we can do. I fancy you're about my Cissy's size. How old are you? 16? No, I don't suppose ya do know (this, as I shook my head, still unable to respond). "Time don't mean nuffin in them gord-forsaken places, I daresay."

The door closed. She was gone. My eyes had got used to the half-light and I realised that I was actually sat up now, on a low bed. There was a chest and a jug of water and washbasin, a chamber pot and an old mirror. I found that I could, at last move. I made my way unsteadily across the room. I needed to make sense of all this. To believe this was really happening to me. Somehow, looking in the tarnished mirror would help. Would verify who I was, to myself at least. I took the mirror back towards the unclear light coming from the window and looked into it. A stranger stared back at me. Some one with wide dark, scared, puffy eyes and hair! Hair that was short, and looked as if it had been hacked off with a knife. Who was this strange woman looking back at me? Surely. Surely this was not happening. My eyes were dark brown, assuredly, and my skin pale but not with bruises and smudges of dirt. And the hair! My hair was a warm golden brown that reflected the sunlight like gold. It fell like a cloak to below my waist when loose, and just above my waist, when braided. This, this creature was not me. Similar eyes and skin, yes. But her hair, my hair, had been shorn off in uneven layers, the front, above my ears, the back slightly longer. It stuck out, greasy, dirty, this was not me! This was not me! I remember hearing a piercing, harrowing scream "My hair. Oh, dear Lord, what have they done to my hair?" I screamed again and again and, gratefully slid into darkness, and forgetfulness.

*　　　　*　　　　*　　　　*　　　　*

"Is it alright Madam?" the hairdresser asked. She had the mirror held behind my head so I could view the cut from behind, as well as look in the mirror in front of me. It was a neat cut and the short length that I had requested. The front framed my face. Perfect for the hot weather that was upon us. I patted my hair, ran my fingers through the shorn locks, hoping that having my hair this short would mean it would last in this style for the summer. That by the time my hair gained its length it would be autumn. Unlike most women, it seemed, I was not one to enjoy a visit to the hairdresser, rather it was to be endured. I wondered why, as I paid and thanked the hairdresser, and left a tip. I walked out into the High Street and the hot summer sunshine.

The market was bustling, full of activity. I decided to treat myself to a cup of coffee, before going home. Sitting at an outside table, stirring my coffee, I watched a spit of chickens turning outside a butcher's shop.

*　　　　*　　　　*　　　　*　　　　*

I recognised the boy who sat and watched the spit, with what seemed to be half a pig, slowly being roasted as the spit turned. His colours were of my brother-in-law's household, a rampaging bull livery broach on his coat. He had worked at The Herber when my father was alive, I was sure. I knew him, and racked my brains, trying to recall the memory. Suddenly we were alone in the kitchen. I gripped the boys wrist as hard as I could and looked as stern as I was able. I had no wish to frighten the lad but I needed his help.

"Who am I?" I asked him. He gaped at me, his mouth open but no sound came out.

"Tell me boy, you know me, do you not?" He nodded. "My name boy, what is it?"

Why?" He tried to brush me off with a jest. "Don't ya know yer own name then?" I gripped him harder and my face became still and serious. Slight I may be but I have dealt with servants all my life. Was used to being obeyed and had on what Papa had called my Madam face on.

I eyed him steadily and then tapped my foot impatiently. "Answer my question, boy. Who am I?"

"You be the Lady Anne Neville." He blurted out.

As relief washed over me others came into the kitchen, the boy was rubbing his wrist. "What be the matter lad?" Jack asked.

"She," the lad jerked his head at me. "She still thinks she be a lady of quality, My Lord's sister-in-law, no less. When all London knows how the Duke of Gloucester visits the Lady Anne near enough every day at The Herber. She, she be mad, mad as a March hare." The whole kitchen roared with their laughter.

"Don't you pay her no mind lad, there's no harm in her, she just be simple, that's all. Now, don't say nowt to no one, do you hear?"

"Nay Jack, course he won't." Maude heaved into view. "Now, run along, youngster, and don't forget to bring us the gossip of the great ones next time you're by."

The youth was gone and with him my only chance, so far, to get a message to Richard. For all my hosts geniality I was watched like a hawk. Was not allowed into the shop but had to work in the kitchen, scouring pans mainly. Maude also had me help her upstairs, once she found I could sew right neatly.

The cap on my head hid my hair, which had begun to grow again, albeit at differing lengths. She had me sewing this evening. They had a large window in their solar, a sign of the prosperity of their pie shop. I was stitching the hem of one of her dresses, when I bethought me to use the scissors I held, not just to cut the thread but also to cut off a lock of my hair. I had no plan, but I wrapped it in a piece of discarded cloth and put it into my bodice.

I slept in the same small room that I had woken up in all those weeks ago. Or was it years? Time seemed to have no meaning. At first I had insisted that I was the Lady Anne Neville and that they should take me to my Lord of

Gloucester, at once. I soon found this was hopeless and but gave rise to laughter, or a slap if I persisted. Maude explained that she had no wish to use me ill but that I'd be 'back' in the mad house if I did not mend my ways. So I pretended to acquiesce and I bided my time until I could escape or get word to Richard. I was watched so closely that the first was nigh impossible, and the second? I had had hope but now, I lay on my bed blinking away my tears. Someone had put a tankard of cheap wine on my dresser, with a piece of beef and some bread. The meat had fat dripping from it, I could not eat, I took the lock of hair from my bodice and putting the grease from the meat on my fingers I fashioned the lock of hair.

Entwined it, so that it became two initials, R. and A. bound together, as Richard had done with my own hair once, when we had met up again, when Edward gained his crown again, after the rebellion it had been a time of great sorrow for my beloved, as well as for me. Father, becoming overly ambitious, had lost his life whilst I was still in France, shackled to the hateful Edward, of Anjou stock, his mother keeping me close until her son gained the English throne. She would not let us bed, though father had insisted on our marriage before he would fight for her. Margaret wanted no Neville child if all went wrong, or my father turned coat, it was the only blessing of the whole sordid affair. All did go wrong. Edward of Lancaster lay dead on the field of battle. Edward of York, knowing I to be a pawn in my father's ambition, gave Richard permission to be in my life, if I wanted him. So I entwined the lock into our initials, and I folded it into the piece of cloth and laid it in my bodice, next to my heart and finally slept.

*   *   *   *   *

"The search continues for people trapped in the recent earthquake, many have been saved, miraculous escapes, but thousands have, unfortunately died."

The news was so harrowing. Natural disasters, they were called but what was natural to claim the lives of so many?

Yet people from all over the world had gone to help clear the rubble, search for survivors, a helping hand across the stench of misery and death. People searching, searching, searching.

*   *   *   *   *

"It be the truth."

I paused at the door leading into the kitchen; the young 'gossip' was back, after only a few days, apparently bursting with news. As I put my hand up to open the latch his next words stopped me.

"The Duke of Gloucester, he marched up the steps of The Herber and hammered on the door, demanding to see the Lady Anne. Said he'd been put off long enough but my Lord, he would not let him in. Then as the Duke turned to go, as has happened every day for a sennight, the Lady Isobel appeared.

"Why Richard," she cries so glad to see him. She runs down the steps and catches his hand. "We are so worried, have you come to help search?"

"Search Isobel?" the Duke asks her "Search for whom?"

"Why Anne, of course." He looks surprised, as well he might.

"Hasn't George told you? Anne has disappeared and all George's efforts to find her have been in vain, I was hoping you had been more successful."

"My Lord of Gloucester, well he cusses quite roundly. Threatens my Lord with many dire threats and gallops off with his retinue around him. Next thing we know, my Lord of Gloucester's men are searching house and tavern, shop and alley, scouring London. Some say he will turn the city upside down and shake it but find my lady Anne he will."

Richard, at last! He was aware of my plight, looking for me. As I stood, trembling, the lad walked through the kitchen door. I grabbed his wrist and yanked him into the cellar before he had time to object.

"What is your name, boy?"

"Richard, what's it to you?"

"Richard, Richard what?"

"Twynyho, Richard Twynyho."

"I knew it," I breathed. "I knew I recognised you." He looked baffled. "You are related to Antoinette? Antoinette Twynyho?" I shook his arm insistently.

"Why, yes." He agreed, "That I be."

"You say that Gloucester looks for the Lady Anne?"

"Ay, he does."

"So." I went on. "How do you think he'll feel if he finds out that one, who could have led him to me, has not done so? Your Aunt," I continued, "was my nurse, and my maid, she would not look kindly to one of her kin doing a disservice to a Neville, and your namesake, My Lord of Gloucester, may reward you well, should you give him this." I gave him the piece of cloth with my lock of hair in it, from my bodice. I gripped him warningly, and spoke firmly. "For he will find me. "T'would be better, if what you say is true Richard Twynyho. T' would be better, me thinks, if it were a shorter, rather than a longer time, for him to find me."

As I let him go he accepted the cloth and its contents and putting it into his doublet was gone, through the shop and out into the street. It was a long shot. But with every stitch I sewed that evening, in the fading light, I said a prayer in my heart.

Bang! The knock on the door was resounding. Waking, not only us, the occupants of the premises behind the pie shop but, from the melee going on in the courtyard leading into the house, most of London as well.

"Open!" A man's voice roared.

"Open! For My Lord of Gloucester."

Panic spread through the house, almost palpable. I in my high garret felt my heart leap, first with excitement and then with dread. It was Richard, come to take me away from this awful place. Come to make me safe but my door was locked, by key and bolt, every night, and I was at the top of the house. Richard would not be looking for the Lady Anne Neville in a garret. He would not find me! He would search and go, forgetting to look in the garret. Not dreaming that his brother, George, Duke of Clarence, could stoop so low; and if he should find me, what then? I had not bathed for months; my hair though growing was lank, greasy and unkempt. My gown was naught but the cheapest cloth. How could I let him see me thus? He would despise me. Not recognise me. Would not know that under the poor cloth and shorn hair was Anne, his Anne, one time playmate and affianced wife.

There was banging and crashing all round the house, with shouts, curses and screams and an occasional, "not here my Lord," as rooms were searched and I was not found. The noise was deafening; they would not hear me if I screamed. But still I did so, beating on the door, screaming his name again and again.

"Richard. Richard. Richard. I'm here. I'm up here. Richard!" Suddenly there was silence and footsteps on the stairs.

His voice, "Anne, is that you?" My voice had gone; I was gasping, shaking. Tears running down my face. My fists beat on the door desperately.

"Stand back," a voice said.

Then, Richard's voice, "Anne, move away from the door."

I moved to my bed. I heard Richard's command. "Open it!"

In a flurry of wood and splinters the lock gave and Richard was in the room. Seeming, as I sat shaking on my bed, to fill it with his very presence. Then he was beside me. I could not stand, because I was shaking so violently. He sat on the bed and carefully turned my face up towards him.

"Oh Anne!" He kissed my mouth softly, then held me to him. Someone brought a long, warm velvet clock and he wrapped it round me. Then, carrying me, like a child as if I weighed nothing. He took me down, down, down the stairs and out under the night sky. I breathed the night air, how sweet freedom smelt and then he was in the saddle of his horse, holding me in front of him. Richard leaned down to someone and pointed to the pie shop and its occupants.

"See to them!" he spoke tersely, unemotional and then we were clattering out of the courtyard.

Safe! At last I was in Richard's arms again, and safe! He held me tightly as I lay swooning in his arms. Suddenly, the horses stopped, a light shone from a doorway, a priest and my old nurse, Antoinette, on the path. Francis lifted me from the saddle, so that Richard could dismount. Francis held me upright, as Richard spoke urgently to the Abbott of St. Martin le Grande. He then came back to me and kissed me gently.

"You be safe now, rest my love, sleep sweetly and let Antoinette see to your needs. I will be back on the morrow, but tonight, tonight I have much to do." He touched my face gently. "Nay love, be not woe begone. We will not be parted again, that I do promise you. The Father Abbott will keep you safe."

Assuredly, my Lord." The Abbott hastened to agree. Then I was led gently in, with Antoinette's arms around me, clucking and crooning as she had when we were babes, into the light and the warmth and the safety of the Abbott's lodgings.

Chapter 10
Norfolk

Little Snoring

The round tower of the church beckoned me as I walked the demesnes of the Manor House father had bought when I was still a babe. He needed a toe- hold in Norfolk and loved Walsingham, which was nearby. We, my family, had changed it into our home so that we missed none of the luxuries of our other mansions or castles. My father had his own retinue and his own hawks and he even appointed the incumbent parish priest. Not his usual practice in his other houses but he had a love of Norfolk and friends here and families who would look out for him with a promise of his Good Lordship.

My mother had her own gardeners, for the garden was her joy and she grew flowers as well as herbs and vegetables for our table. Strips of tilled land boasted wheat and barley and corn. There were orchards that grew apples and pears and plums and of course the beehives for honey were also housed deep amongst the fruit trees. It was warm, sunny and pretty much like heaven to me.

I remembered the last visit, before going to Warwick and our flight to Devon and on to Calais. A dark, stormy night, with my sister crying out in pain as she was jolted along with only myself and a maid to aid her. She had cried out every time the litter hit a rut in the road, which was all the time. Until even my patience was wearing thin, though I knew she was near her time and in severe discomfort. Again my mother tried to persuade father to let Isobel and I stay here, at Warwick, the King would not harm us and here Isobel could be brought to bed safely.

My father had been adamant, a change of horses for those men who had ridden even farther than we, and whose nags where dropping with fatigue. Only they had a brief respite and then we were urged on by my father, on to where his own ships awaited us in harbour, a nightmare ride, south to Exeter. Ships which had been readied by his own men, sent swiftly on ahead, whilst he had come to get us from Warwick. I was back at Bowles in Norfolk with Richard! Now the horrors were over. My father was dead and I had been married to my own lord, in St. Stephen's Chapel, some weeks ago. We had come to pay our respects at the shrine of Our Lady of Walsingham and to stop, on our way north, at the manors of Bowles and Walcote at Little Snoring. All fathers' lands had gone to

George of course but Richard had been granted my father's manors and desmesnes north of the Trent.

The sunlight lit the round tower and indeed the whole church and the face over the tower door stared at me daring me to go in. Once the round tower had been part of a Saxon church, but we Norman's had re-built a newer more modern church, but kept the tower, which housed some fine bells. They hung silent now but they had pealed out many times in our sojourn at the manor calling the villagers and us, to church. My father had loved to worship at the church and knew the villagers by name, as he did at all his own houses and castles. It was part of his charm and they all loved him for it and his generosity. I left the tower and entered the church by its new Norman door, it had a deep cool porch, and the inner door was shut. I gripped the handle firmly and turned it, slowly the heavy oak door, well oiled, gave to my push and I found myself standing on a familiar stone flagged floor.

*   *   *   *   *

Not one of us knew where we were going and we followed the some times inaccurate, twist and turns on the map. It was evening and we were both tired but I felt determined to at least call in to the church and `get a feeling of the surrounding countryside. I had not believed it when I read in the latest book I had bought about Richard III that a Neville manor was at Little Snoring in Norfolk. This was a line of enquiry of which I could not let go.

We had looked at the map when we had planned our day out. Walsingham was somewhere we liked to visit and Little Snoring was only 'round the corner' or that is how it had looked on the map. Now, after turning up little country roads that led nowhere I was not so sure. The road signs were confusing to say the least, so we asked, and were directed to a left-hand fork. It led to a church all right but not Little Snoring's church. Undaunted we backed up the road and continued. There, in the distance, I saw a round tower.

"That's it, that's it." I cried out excited now. "It can't be far, just round the corner". In reality, of course, I had no idea if this was indeed the church we sought. On the premise that every village has a church, we just aimed to find the church first and if they still existed, the Manors, which had once belonged to the Neville's. The tower looked promising, and we halted outside the gateway of the Norman church with a round tower off to its left side as we looked towards the front doorway. We got out to investigate further. No sign of any type of manor house was near, leave alone one that the mighty Neville's might have built but neither had there been when we first visited Sherriff Hutton. The chances were high that any residential manor house had been demolished or burnt down years ago, as had been the fate of so many. Again I thought of Sherriff Hutton, where a few fingers of building were all that was left of a once mighty manor house. The church in Little Snoring however did still stand, as churches tended to from the Norman era, the round tower was not attached to the church however but stood off to one side by the front door of the church itself.

'Very unusual,' I thought, the church itself was obviously Norman, but why would the Saxon round tower be left? The answer seemed to present itself in the fact that the tower held three bells, 'possibly', I thought 'the round tower had been left to be used as a bell tower.' Rather than add on the Norman church to the English original, as so many Norman churches did, the original church seemed to have been demolished, all but its round tower and a new Norman church built in its stead. I walked up to the wooden door, turned the handle, and walked in.

*   *   *   *   *

As always there were flowers from our gardens decorating the church. Lilies by the altar and honeysuckle complimenting the sunlight that streamed through the stained glass windows. Rushes on the floor had lavender strewn in amongst them to give off its sweet scent and the evening air smelt sweetly of the flowers adorning God's house. The stained glass lit up the muted colours on the church walls. I made my way up the aisle, towards the nave, my patens echoing on the flagstones. I knelt at the altar rail and gave thanks to God for leading me to this safe haven out of the trials and tribulations of the past year. Only a year, yet I had grown physically and mentally, into a woman, leaving my childhood behind.

The village church was small, but my father did it proud during his lifetime, even engaging the incumbent Vicar to take care of the little flock who worshipped there. The church was kept worthy of the Neville presence that occasionally graced it.

My father had given gifts of gold and velvet and robes for the priest, that he would not be ashamed to wear. Yes he had been generous, so generous, which is why the people loved him but his ambition laced with greed had been his undoing. I sighed and asked for God's blessing, and the sun sent a rainbow of colours across the white altar cloth bathing all in light and colour.

*   *   *   *   *

The worn flagstones were cold underfoot, despite my trainers. Old gravestones peered out from under raised pews, which did not look very old. "I wonder when these were put in?" I said, "they cover the grave stones so they could be Victorian, certainly not original." The church was very bare and the windows, though the plasterwork was ornate, the glass was clear. Another church that had suffered at the hands of Henry VIII's dissolution of the monasteries and the destruction of so many churches. Even a small church, like this, had not escaped. But then if it had been Neville land, as a Yorkist church and village any destruction by the Tudor Monarch would not be surprising. I walked up to the altar rail, though plain I felt the history of the church, almost palpable. It seemed that people would appear at any moment.

*   *   *   *   *

"Anne." A low, well-spoken, well-modulated voice broke in on my prayer. A voice I recognised from my last few happier visits, before we had run to Calais and the France and into the arms of Lancaster. It was John Hogeson, the last incumbent my father had installed at the church, I blushed as I looked at him. I was aware what all the changes in the Neville fortune might bring to this good and faithful man. The last time we had met I had still been a girl, now I was a woman grown and married too, and, I smiled to myself, with child too.

"Father, please excuse me, I had thought I was alone, I had thought." I paused, "That the King would be concerned about who was the incumbent of this little Church?" he asked. I nodded. I had no wish to see any of father's retainers or friends, suffer because of his unwise actions.

"Do not worry, my child, Edward has not seen fit to remove me from my post, as yet." His voice smiled. "But you are no longer a child Anne, look at you, you're a woman grown, and married I hear." I nodded, glowing.

He too nodded, "Enceinte, my dear?" he asked gently. I blushed and nodded. How could he tell I asked, at that he laughed. "Vicars have many a parishioner who has been great with child. I am not stranger to childbed, my dear." He smiled again, "Come. I have no wish to embarrass you. Are you happy?" I nodded again, smiling into his eyes, "Ay he said, I can see for myself you are. Long may it last my dear a long and happy life to you all." And he signed the cross over my forehead.

I left the church and walked all round it. The rays of the setting sun bathing it in light. I tried to imagine where the Neville mansion would have been, over that slight rise perhaps? If so there was no trace and no mention of it in the booklet I had bought about the History of the Church. I left; he was waiting for me in the car; vowing to find out more. Fakenham, the King's manor extended to Little Snoring, so there just might be a chance of finding out more about how it had looked in the 15th century. I turned and looked back as we drove away the sun behind the round tower with its rays like a halo of light around it.

"The sun in splendour," I murmured, "What?" he queried, I shook my head and settled down to read the booklet on my lap, as we drove home.

* * * * *

Crowland

"I've never seen anything like this before! Look at this brickwork! The stone! I bet this was all water, under here, it must have been!"

The heart of the fen country, Croyland, or Crowland, we hadn't known what to expect. The bridge, Trinity Bridge, was wonderful in itself and Crowland a lovely village. We, however, were heading for the Abbey, Croyland Abbey. As with a lot of the abbeys in Norfolk and the fen country we knew it was both ancient and historic. The famous Chronicles had been written here, as had the continuations, the author of these last two inputs being unknown. We headed towards the Abbey.

The horses pranced and their bridles jingled in the crisp, frosty air. We were wrapped up against an early frost, the autumn sun struggling to get through and warm the earth. Village chimneys smoked as peat fires burnt in the early morning. The clattering of our horse's hooves on the bridge meant the curious eyes of the villagers and their children. Richard and I had chosen to spend time travelling to the Estates which once had been my father's and now belonged to Richard and also myself, now we were married. Edward had given my father's land north of the Trent to Richard, for his loyalty. Now we were going home, to Middleham, via our estates and visiting friends and shrines on the way.

Richard and I wanted to continue the good stewardship that had been installed in my father's time and to enjoy our journey home, as husband and wife. So we had visited Walsingham's shrine whilst staying at the Manor in Little Snoring, which my father had bought in times past. Now we were at Croyland.

The Abbey itself was a beautifully crafted building and we stayed with the Abbott in his lodgings, far more luxurious accommodation than the cells, and the dortoire, for the monks who resided there. Now, rested and with the delight of the hunt in front of us, we clattered over the Trinity Bridge, our horse champing at their bits, falcons hooded, on their handlers wrists, on through the village to greet the morning sun and fly the birds.

The stonework of the Abbey was magnificent. We paused to take in the detail of the huge arched doorway. Still standing as it must have, when it was first built, the detail was amazing and so was the sculpting, of the figures and the ornamentation. The church part of the Abbey was still in use and decorated for a wedding, so we looked around here first. Then into the ruins to view further the magnificence of the archways. One arch looking as if nothing was holding it up and that gravity would soon win the battle and cause it to come crashing to earth.

We had had brought a picnic with us and we sat on the grass, amongst the daisies and buttercups, trying to imagine the splendour, which had long gone.

Norwich

I had a whole three hours to indulge myself, whilst he went into the Art School, Cathedral or Castle? Choices! Really though I felt that there was no choice, it had to be the Castle. We had both visited the Cathedral on a number of occasions, so the Castle it was. I walked up the steps in the side of the bank and arrived at the 'front door'. I smiled to myself at my mental terminology. How could a Castle have a front door? Locked! Blow, it was 9.30 a.m. and did not open until 10. Oh well! A walk around 'the grounds', which is really the glass dome of the shopping mall, seemed to be in order. I wondered if I could get inside and grab a cup of coffee whilst I waited? I walked round the dome, admired the water feature. I could see an exit into the place but no entrance, as I did not have long to wait I did not worry; I decided to sit by the water feature and enjoy the sunshine. Suddenly it was 10 o'clock. I decided to approach the Castle by the main gate, which looked like a tarmac drawbridge.

*   *   *   *   *

The mound that the Castle stood upon was huge; it seemed to tower above me. I stared up at the Castle completely over awed. I shook myself, took a deep breath, I could not show how I felt, I wasn't just Lady Anne Neville anymore, I was not only Richard's wife, but his Queen, Queen of England.

My head straightened, my shoulders went back, and I gathered my skirts and prepared to alight from the horse litter.

*   *   *   *   *

Chapter 11
In Chancery

It was a cold, wet, drizzle. In fact the whole holiday was marked by the wet weather. Flooding had ruined the week for the families who were camping, their week ruined; at least we had a caravan.

So here we were, supporting two people, joining the queue into Pembroke Castle, trying, hoping, it would be of interest and pass the time in a pleasant and enjoyable way for the two men in our care.

There was a tour but we elected to wander round the Castle with only the guide book, knowing 'our men' would not care to be huddled from room to room, area to area with a group of strangers. Parts of the Castle were in a good state of repair. The chambers in the Tower where Margaret Beaufort (Tudor) had, it was thought given birth to her son Henry. She was in Pembroke for her son's birth, being sheltered by her brother-in-law, Jasper Tudor, after her husband's death. Jasper had shown concern for his nephew from this time, and throughout his life.

The incident was just part of the long history of Pembroke Castle, but I was surprised at how little was made of the birth of the welsh man who became King of England. I was surprised at the positive lack of enthusiasm, it was not what I had expected after reading many books about this era of history. It was apparently not a fact that Henry Tudor had been born here, just a 'maybe'. There was a tableau of figures depicting how people may have lived at this time, a room, a bed and that was all. Then we were out in the mizzle again looking round the part of the Castle, which was now in ruins.

We walked through to an area marked 'Chancery' on the wall plaque. I could not find it in the guide and I asked my co-worker if she knew what it was, what the word Chancery meant. She did not, however and we moved on, I still thumbing through the guidebook, to no avail.

"Chancery." I looked up, one of the men we were supporting had spoken. He ran his hands along and down a wall, "Chancery" he repeated.

"I wonder what it means?" I said.

"It was the court." Came his reply."

"Was it Philip?"

"Where they judged the thieves and murderers," he said. I pressed home this awakening, "You know this place don't you Philip? I asked. He smiled, "What were you Philip, a rascal or on the bench?" He smiled again a deep smile of recognition of who he had been. "You where on the bench Philip, weren't you?" I stated. "You old rogue Philip, you were a judge, Philip you were on the bench."

His smile broadened and he turned away one hand still caressing the stone wall. I wanted to ask more but the light had gone as suddenly as it had come. His pleasure in being in the Castle, however, remained until we left.

Chapter 12

Travail

The nursery was always warm. In winter a huge fire was kept burning all day. Turfed at night to stop the coals dying, it would be brought back to life each morning. Still dark, the maid would be in to coax the flames, as she helped me to dress, a lad would bring logs up for one of the serving girls to add to the fire, to keep it burning. The nursery was, of course in a separate tower to the main living area of the Castle and the Great Hall.

My lord entertained much at Warwick and there was much to-ing and fro-ing. Not right for the young one to be bothered by the noise, or for my lord and lady to have to worry about the cries of their daughter.

But we also had quiet times when my lord was at Court, or off visiting his father, uncle and cousins. Now Isabel was born my lady stayed at home more and beside there was much going on that it was not safe for her to be caught up in.

She could not carry boys, it seemed, for every child she lost, was male. Yet another daughter was born, in time, too much rejoicing by my lord. Strange, as we thought he would be desperate for a male heir. Yet he seemed cheerful enough, bidding my lady to also be of good cheer, they would fix fine marriages for these daughters. They would be his heirs and who knew what the future held for them all?

*   *   *   *   *

Anne Beachamp

What had happened to my husband? The closeness we had once felt appeared to be gone. Now there was only pride and ambition.

I protested, of course I did. No need for us to run from Edward. No matter what, our King did not make war on women and children or babes and our eldest daughter was about to drop her first born. It was a critical time, only days away, we could not go galloping across England to take ship, with our eldest girl so near her time. Anne also but still a child, should not be dragged from our safe Warwick to God knows where!

"Calais!" he exclaimed, exultingly, still so sure that the next throw of the die would all come up for him. "Wenlock will shelter us at Calais, he is my own man and there we will re-group and return to England."

"To do what?" I asked him. "Richard, tell me, surly you do not propose all out rebellion against Edward? Richard, please, think what you are doing, what the outcome will be for us all? Edward may be our cousin, but his is also our King, he would not, could not, forgive again."

"Bah! Edward and who is Edward without Warwick? Popinjay, who does he think he is, well he's gone too far this time, far too far!" He drew his brows together in a deep frown.

I tried again to reason with him. To point out that Edward was our King. If he had faults, well so had we all but Edward, as King, could expect his to be overlooked, could expect our loyalty. We had fought for the Yorkshire rose all our adult lives, yes, Richard had been pushed to rebel, I understood that, but Ned had remained King, through it all, Warwick had never sought to topple York from the throne.

It was different now, he said and he paced our bedroom as I tried to dress, my agitation showing as I fumbled my clothes into place. He had sent my maid away, with the pretext of her helping Isabel and Anne but I knew that he wanted no prying eyes or ears to our conversation. Laughing suddenly he helped me dress, and I relaxed against him, this was my Richard, not the other man who had paced so violently but the moment went, as suddenly as it had come.

"This time," he gleamed at me, "this time I will topple Ned off the throne I gave him. There are others alive who might yet wear the Crown." I looked at him in horror as the realisation of what he intended dawned on me. "Lancaster?" I breathed. It could not be, he would not side with those who had killed, father, Uncle, cousins. "Yes." His smile was triumphant. "I will defeat Edward and put the crown back on Henry VI's rightful head." I was in a daze, could not believe what my husband was saying.

Suddenly, it seemed, we were ready. In boots and warm riding dresses, cloaks of good wool and leather riding gloves, the horse stamped impatiently ready to be off. The horse litter was to take Isabel and Anne. Not that Anne could not ride with the best of us, but one look at her stricken face and her sister's equally stricken and afraid for her baby, led their father to agree, they could ride together, for comfort one to the other. For speed the rest of us were on horseback. I rode as close to the litter as I dared in the dark, listening for any signs of imminent labour from Isabel. The windows had been closed with heavy curtains and bedding laid on the floor and seat but I could still hear Isabel's groans mixed in with the hoof-beats as we plunged through the dark, lanterns barely lighting the way.

Chapter 13

France

The wimple chaffed my neck and chin, it was a cheap, harsh material. The Queen, ex-Queen, I corrected myself, now a prisoner with myself, could no longer demand fine damask. She could, however, and did demand I wear the wimple, symbol of my widowhood. Her son, her boy, her star was dead and she mourned accordingly, and I? I, who had never been a true wife to him, who never cared for him nor he for me; was made to wear the widow's garb.

I had lived, after my marriage to her son, with Margaret. She had not been cruel but kindness was a word not known to her. She could not bend or bow. Her son had been brought up by her and was the same, except that he thought cruelty a fine game. He used me to lash, with his tongue and for his cruel remarks to hurt and wound. I did not even have my own apartments to hide away in and gain some peace. The only peace was in front of my Prie Dieu and my only comfort.

We were man and wife yet kept separate by Margaret. She wanted no Neville brood if my father played her false, as heir to her son's throne. She did not know that I silently thanked her for this mercy. To her, her son was all. To me, he was an athema. Living in her apartments, my bedroom next to hers, no privacy was allowed me. She would sweep into my room un-announced and even she if she saw I was at prayer would retreat noisily.

Now my father, the great Kingmaker himself, was dead! My husband taunted me with his fate and our now imminent divorce. Once King he wanted no Neville wife. Things had gone wrong, however, badly wrong and Edward IV had forced Margaret to stop running and do battle, at Tewkesbury. A nearby Abbey, Cerne, was our shelter and here they brought her the news, the loss of the battle and the loss of the Lancastrians cause, with her son's death.

Apparently he died fighting bravely, no comfort to Margaret, who had collapsed on hearing the news. She then withdrew into her royal dignity, and would allow no one near to comfort her.

I felt caught between two stools. Not wanting my husband, yet not able to delight either in his death, or his mother's grief. My father would have called me soft but my mother would have understood. We had been separated on our return to England and for her own safety she now mourned my beloved father behind Abbey walls. How could she do otherwise? Edward would not keep on forgiving my father's treachery, for not only had he raised arms against his sovereign, he had also produced the Lancastrian heir to place on England's throne. No Edward could not forgive this and we did not expect mercy. Isabel, at least was safe, married to the King's brother, who despite his numerous treacherous and traitorous deeds, seemed to lead a charmed life and had again been forgiven. Inheriting through his marriage, most of my father's lands, though not his title, George was still Clarence, not Warwick.

I knew not my own fate. A fate brought to me but not of my wish. Suddenly we had been taken to France, Isabel losing her first born whilst our ships lay off Calais. My father then hatched his plot with the Anjou woman. Going down on his knees to beg forgiveness and to plead a pact, to de-throne his ungrateful and ungracious sovereign. She heard him out. Making him beg, watching his pain as he knelt before her.

She had had to relent, to side with the man who had previously plucked the throne from her husband and her son. So that she hid with that son, in France, a fugitive and her husband, more monk than King, languished in the Tower Palace, a prisoner to all intents and purposes.

Then I, a pawn in their deadly game was put forward as wife to her son. I, who had been promised to Richard, was to be forced into an unwelcome marriage with the enemy. For we had always been for York and he was Lancaster.

I remember my father telling me of his plans, in which I was to play so vital a role. He sat me down in front of a huge fire and I watched the flames play and dance round the logs, not wanting to hear how my life had been re-ordered. How I was to direct the new King from one side whilst my father did the same from the other. Edward of Lancaster presumably trapped in the middle, with no will of his own to gainsay the Kingmaker. But I was no Margaret and Edward was not his father. He was opinionated and knew what he wanted and where he was going, neither Margaret nor her son, where happy to include the Neville brood in their plans.

I tried to tell my father. Tried to explain. Tried to turn the tide from the way it was going, all to no avail. The plans had been made. No damsel; whose opinion mattered naught, only that she obey her father's wishes; was going to prevent the Kingmaker's grandson from being King.

Isabel and George were furious when they were told of the change in my father's plans. "What about me?" George had fumed, "I was supposed to be

King, I am Edward's heir," but not Henry's and my father was now for Lancaster not York. He spoke to George, soothed him with words and promises but I saw George's face and watched him chew his upper lip to prevent his red-hot lava of anger from flowing. Biding his time he would travel back to England to fight with my father but I knew that George was now lost to my father's cause. He would turn coat again and side with Edward, his brother, if the luck of the die changed. My sister Isabel said as much before they left, and George? George spat venom at me, telling me he would be revenged on me yet.

"I'll make sure no Neville sibling sits on England's throne if it be not Isabel!" He showed my father a smooth brow, however, and a smiling countenance and stood behind me with Isabel at the betrothal ceremony.

When I first met Edward of Lancaster I was pleasantly surprised. He was tall and fair to look at. Not many years older than myself, I thought, maybe I can make this work. He seemed to like what he saw too. Bowing low to me and speaking softly when we met, bringing me sweetmeats and wine. My father beamed and took ship for England. From then my life changed. My mother was kept to the apartments she had shared with my father and I, now betrothed, was in the care of Lancaster.

We had all been together that last night and in the morning my mother and sister had helped the tire women to dress me in my betrothal gown. My hair long and thick, with auburn lights was left loose, and flowers were worked in with gems brought by my father and the jeweller fitted them into my hair. He had cunningly wrought a tiara to hold the gems from long stems of golden silk the flowers held by 'invisible' hairpins fitted into my hair. The tiara of diamonds and yellow sapphires held my hair back from my face, looking, in my father's eyes like the queen he would have me be. My mother fussed and interfered, making sure all was done for good luck and happiness leading to a fertile marriage bed.

It felt like a dream that was not happening to me but to someone else. I tried to be happy, for my father's sake, happy to be so important to his plans. But I had lived so long with the certainty of marrying Richard that this new uncertainty, which was changing my life, though exciting, scared me. I prayed and thanked God that Margaret had taught her son well. His manner and speech had been impeccable. It had been made plain that although he had his own apartments I would lodge with my mother-in-law. I knew the reasons and did not mind. If truth be told I was relieved, it would give us time, myself and Edward, to get to know one another, to be friends as well as husband and wife.

After the ceremony was feasting and dancing and I was happily dreaming of a pleasant marriage when the real Edward confronted me in his mother's solar, where we were allowed to meet and talk, once I was ready for bed. I was not ready for his sneering face and cruel jibes. He left me in no doubt as to my role in his life. It was convenience, nothing more, a contract forced by necessity.

He would come to my bed once he was King in order to have children. Meanwhile he would keep his own council. I need not expect to have any say at all, either before or after he was King. He would expect me to watch floggings, hangings or executions with him. Otherwise, I was to understand, that his mother meant all to him, he would be guided by her and her alone. I need not think to write to my father, I was not allowed to send nor receive letters. He spoke without drawing breath, or so it seemed. Then, mockingly he changed back to the courtier, as he had been when first we met. Calling me 'My Lady' he offered me his arm to escort me to my chamber. I took it, unquestioning feeling and no doubt looking dazed by his volte farce. He led me to my bed and bade me goodnight, bowing low and kissing my hand. Then he kissed my cheeks and hissed, "remember," at me from between his teeth and left, bidding my tire women to 'take good care of me' had he said 'guard her well' it would have sounded the same.

The bed was turned down and had been warmed but I shivered as I climbed in between the sheets. I lay, dry eyed, feeling helpless for the first time. I knew I was indeed helpless in their Lancastrian hands. Unable to communicate with family or friends, even my mother's visits would be watched. I thought of Middleham and of Richard, my eyes wide with staring out of the window, I watched until at long last the rosy fingers of the sun appeared, and as the sun rose, exhausted I slept.

*   *   *   *   *

Changes

I awoke with a start but feeling warm, comfortable, safe for a moment. All fled as I recognised my new room and remembered the words of my bridegroom. My mother, in her own apartments, my father en route back to England with George and my sister, Isabel, not allowed to communicate with them, I was to be a virtual prisoner.

She was not cruel, Margaret, I was just watched every minute of the day and night. We walked together in the gardens but I was never allowed to walk alone. Yet as long as my husband kept his distance I was content. He visited his mother of course but I was not allowed to be part of their conversations or thoughts. Truly I was glad. For at these times I only had a servant with me and I would stitch and embroider edgings for our sleeves to brighten up old dresses, for we still had to economise. Louis' help was for mercenaries to fight for England's throne, not for women's fripperies. Often I would read in the library, laying a book out on the desks, the sun streaming through the windows or the rain pattering an echo to my loneliness and my private thoughts of the good times at Middleham and Richard.

I found my husband true to his word when it came to my having to watch as his servants were punished and he chose every opportunity to punish. He seemed to take a perverse delight in their pain. A child from the scullery, or a serving man who had somehow annoyed him, or had fallen short of Edward's standards, as these changed daily this was not hard to do. So he made me stand or sit by him. Nor was I allowed to turn away but he could not prevent me from closing my eyes. Although, even then, he would twist my braids in his hands and jerk my head so fiercely that I opened my eyes with pain.

It was a relief when he begged his mother to be allowed to join the battle force being raised in England, by my father. I thought of the joy of him simply not being there. But no, Margaret and I and my mother would all sail for England and the Duke of Somerset was to watch over him. For if the prince died then so did all their hopes.

The one joy was being with my mother. She too had been kept a virtual prisoner. Unable to leave her apartments and wander at will. Her attempts to visit me had been prevented, even the maids having the gall to turn her away at my door. Although we knew that the orders must have been Margaret's.

Now, all riding for the coast, we were able to at least be in one another's company. We were putting up in an Inn for the night when news came of my father's success at raising troops. His popularity had proved invaluable as he swept all before him. York was in flight with his brother of Gloucester, to Burgundy and Henry VI proclaimed again the true King. Margaret was exultant, they must hurry to England. Ships must be organised, her laggardly journey was now of supreme importance. Despite our fears, mother and I could not but be pleased at father's victories and whilst he was victorious, we were treated with grudging respect.

In private I worried, not about Ned but about Richard. We had no desire, mother and I, to be thrust into court life under Lancastrian rule. Nor did I relish the idea of being Princess of Wales with Edward as my Prince, one-day to rule England. What did Edward or I know of how to rule a country? Though my job would be to produce heirs, now father had secured the throne for Lancaster.

Margaret, of course, would rule through her husband and then with her son once her husband died, a role she was used to playing during Henry's years as King. I groaned inwardly as I remembered the previous battles, now handed down to children as folklore. Of the Lancastrian armies ravaging the countryside as they swept down on London, how London had closed its gates to them and Margaret had turned north.

My father and Ned had been welcomed in London and Ned declared King. It had been ten years ago and I but 5 years of age, Isabel had been 10 years old, the same age as Richard and George 13. The two boys had been sent to Burgundy and now ten years later, two brothers once again fled to Burgundy. The two brothers this time however, were Richard and Ned. Oh God! I prayed for their safety as I wondered what my father's ambition had led him to unleash in England.

*   *   *   *   *

Tewkesbury

The weather was against us; time and again we had tried to embark to no avail. The sea was treacherous, storms raced across the sky and the wind howled ceaselessly. Margaret may have risked us, but not her precious son. We had no more news of the progress in England. Whether the country was won to my husband's side or lost. Margaret was adamant; her husband was back on England's throne. Ruling, with Warwick by his side the Lancastrian cause was invincible. But I had seen my lord challenge Ned before, and lose. I silently wondered, and prayed, not for Lancaster but for Richard, my Lord. At last we set sail. We had hated the waiting but at least Anne and I had been able to have contact in the small inn. Now I was put on to a separate ship, the voyage home, for me was to hold no comfort aboard, only the hope of my husbands victory and his arms, once more about me, could sustain me until we reached England.

That and prayer for both my children and, dare I think it, for Ned and Richard, especially Richard who had become so dear to me at Middleham.

        *   *   *   *   *

The waiting was over, and our ships embarked, and Margaret in a last cruel gesture, had once more separated mother and I. We were to journey home separately. All I had prayed for was to go home, yet home, for me was Middleham, and I knew that my chances of seeing it again were slight. The sea was rough, so rough that our ships were separated and my mother's ship was lost from our sight. I knew not whether she would land in safe harbour or be taken by the sea.

Our ship docked safely in Weymouth, Kent, and we were met by the Duke of Somerset and Courtney, the Earl of Devonshire, who recommended that we move on to St Mary's Abbey. An inn was found where we might rest and this at least was warm and rooms were made ready for us.

Margaret was anxious for news. Where was Warwick's messenger? Food was laid before us, and we all ate, even Margaret for she must have been as cold as the rest of us. We had gone to bed when my father's messenger arrived, at last. Sleepily we went down to the Parlour to hear how my father did.

The man was bespattered with mud. He had heard news of our landing. Scouts had been posted to bring him word and he had come, straight away, hence his arriving so late. He paused and Margaret tapped her foot impatiently. All she wanted was word from Warwick; she did not need this preamble. In her agitation she had not noticed that the messenger was one of my father's friends, Lord Scrope of Bolton, or that he held out no parchment for her to take and read. I, standing to one side, did notice and a feeling of fear and foreboding touched my heart. I moved forward, as Margaret demanded news and I saw his eyes fill with tears, which coursed down his cheeks. The dreaded moment had come and I moved towards her, to comfort, but Margaret stayed me with her hand.

"Come my Lord," she spoke imperiously, "since you carry no message for me to read, impart me your news."

"Warwick is dead, My Lady." There were gasps from all in the room, except Margaret.

"Dead, dead! How can he be dead? He had my husband brought from the Tower. The Yorkist's fled. Henry is again King. There must be some mistake. Tell me, tell me all." At last she sat. Her men closed around her and I heard his words, as I stood, rooted to the spot, unnoticed and unable to move.

"The King is back." Margaret winced at the title he unwittingly gave Ned. "He and his brother," (my heart leaped, Richard,) "they landed at Ravenspur a sennight since and marched unopposed through England. At first no one seemed to care but gradually more and more Lords and men joined his army. My Lord of Warwick had gathered his forces at Coventry, and waited within the wall for my Lord of Clarence to join him." He paused. "Clarence arrived with ten thousand men but on seeing his brother's and their army, did sue for a truce. My Lord of Gloucester rode to meet him and after some words Clarence rode back with Gloucester to the King his brother and there, so we heard, he did beg forgiveness on one knee. Edward agreed of course, it could only make his claim stronger. The armies joined and they set off for London." He paused again and some one handed him a flagon of wine, from which he drank deeply. He had ridden hard and Margaret had still not allowed him to sit.

"The King, Edward IV, Madam," he looked at her apologetically, "Brought his wife, and new-born son out of sanctuary at Westminster. We heard that the citizens cheered themselves hoarse."

Margaret frowned, she tapped her foot angrily, she needed no reminding of Ned's popularity. "Go on." She said tersely.

"The final battle was at Barnet, My Lady. A fog came down and our two armies over stretched each other. Gloucester led their right flank and had to struggle down a steep wooded hill before he could engage in battle and we had a small force climb up through the trees to harry his men to stop them reaching our main army. Meanwhile de Vere routed the left flank and just as we thought we had won, Oxford returned, his livery blazoning the shooting star," he paused again.

"And?" Margaret queried?

"And our men thought the shooting star was Edward's Sunne in Splendour. Other's that, because de Vere's troops came towards them; that he had joined his wife's family, and shouts of 'treason' were heard. In the confusion our own troops cut down my Lord of Oxford's men. There was a rout!" He shrugged expressively. I do not know how I got to be standing in front of him. Suddenly, I was there, my hand on his shoulders, as he knelt.

"My father?" It was barely a whisper. He saw me, for the first time, and standing, returned my gesture. "My Lady Anne? Oh, My Lady. That was the pity of it. Your father survived the battle. Bloodied yes and tired, he got separated from the rest of us; we think he sought his horse. The enemy host must have seen him and thought to take a great prize. He fought them, laid about him with his great sword, ay and killed many too, for we found them with his body.

He was sore wounded, My Lady and this last skirmish it was that killed him. We found him, stripped of his helm and shield. Likely they did not even know him or recognise his coat of arms. He held me, as I sobbed. "If they thought to profit from it, they did not for the King came, calling his name and though we ran, we saw him kneel at your father's side and call down curses on those who had disobeyed his orders and killed his noble cousin."

I know not how my mother received the news. Only that the Abbey she had sought shelter in, on landing in England, gave her comfort in her grief. I could not go to her and she knew she would not be allowed near me now my father, our only protector, was dead. Margaret would have no sympathy for us, only anger that her cause, her son's fight for England's throne, had so badly gone awry. So it was that we were forced march across England to try and cross the Severn into Wales. There Jasper Tudor promised us protection, somewhere to re-group and for the Lancastrian heir to make another bid for his throne. We never got to Wales but were stayed, by Ned, to fight at Tewkesbury, where Margaret and I were to await the outcome the guests of nearby Cerne abbey. This then was how we came to the last throw of the die and all the while, none talked of Gloucester or whether he lived or died. My prie dieu and my knees saw hard work at these perilous times.

Then it came, the news that the battle was won, by Edward and Richard. My husband, her son, was dead, killed in battle, fighting valiantly we were told and we were prisoners of the crown.

I did not mind now I was free of being watched by Margaret or one of her attendants. Now I could only try to give her comfort, though for her there was none to be had. Her husband was back in the Tower. I did not care. I saw my life in ruins about me. Forced into a marriage that had been no marriage, what would life hold in store now? Tainted by the Lancastrians, Ned would see me as his enemy and Richard? Who knew what Richard would feel? He, whose motto attested to his feelings about loyalty. 'Loyaltie me lie' (Loyalty binds me), he would want naught to do with me now. Margaret forced me to wear the wimple, to signify her loss and my widowhood to all, it chaffed my skin, I hated it.

Chapter 14
The Tower

There was a clatter of hooves in the courtyard and I ran to the window. "Madame," I said to Margaret, "it is the King." Her face was immobile, whilst I felt my heart fill with dread. Richard had told me all about his brother, Ned. But of King Edward IV I knew naught. All I did know was that forgiveness would not enter the room with the King who had paraded Margaret through London.

There was a loud bang on the door and someone announced, "His Majesty, King…" the rest was lost as Edward strode into the room, sweeping all out of his way. He ignored me, as I dropped to a full curtsey, and walked straight up to Margaret.

"Madame," he said, "we grieve for you the loss of your son and husband. You will of course remain our prisoner until such time as we can decide what to do with you." Then, somewhat kindlier, as her stricken face still showed no sign, "you will be royally housed, in the tower, Madame, York does not make war on women, OR children." He emphasised the last. Memories no doubt of his brother, Edmund, who was murdered by her Lancastrian troops and to show that her son had died in battle, not murdered as she stormed when e'er she did speak of it. She had the grace to flush at this, and to thank Edward quietly and with dignity. He turned to go. I thought he would leave without seeing me, without pronouncing my sentence. I looked up, my mouth opening, what would I say?

What would I implore? I lowered my eyes; no I had no rights in this. Then he stopped in front of me. "Cousin Anne?" He queried and I nodded, then, quickly, caught his hand and kissed his coronation ring.

"Fealty?" he drawled raising an eyebrow, "from a Neville?"

"My sister is a Neville too my Lord"

"Ay," his brow darkened, "and married to my brother, not a wise reminder mayhap." Then he smiled suddenly, "Did you wish to ask something?" I nodded again, and spoke, my voice trembling, "Richard?" I said and then corrected myself, (how many more blunders would I make I chided myself) "My Lord of Gloucester, he is well?" He looked at me closely now, then bent and swiftly loosed the wimple and let it fall to the ground.

"I had forgot," he said, "how young you are." Then strode to the door, "we will send our brother to you my Lady. "He and I will decide your fate." The door closed and he was gone.

Suddenly, locked in the Tower palace with Margaret, I could mourn my father. His death becoming more real as my fortunes changed with hers. She mourned her son but though my tears mingled with hers, I, in reality, mourned my father, the great Kingmaker. I was now truly alone, with no one to offer me protection. Stripped of my inheritance, which had been given to George and Richard.

My mother hiding in a convent had had her goods taken as if she too were dead. We, who had been unwilling pawns, drawn into the Lancastrian cause.

Drawn into their last throw of the die by my father, were now left, stranded. My father was truly gone. No more would he stride the halls of power, command men's loyalties and protect his family. My sister, at least, was safe being married to George. My mother and I were stranded, by my father's death and by fate. I had railed against my part in his plans but now he was gone, would have gladly accepted my role to have him back.

I had trusted in him to bring my husband and Margaret under his control. Which would, in turn, I had hoped, improve my married life. His loss was an ache in my breast and like Margaret, dry of tears at last, I too sat before the fire at night, or gazed out into the gardens by day, blindly and in pain at my loss. He had always been there and now was gone. Of my fate I knew not and alone now, did not greatly care, for if he were dead what was left in my life, what truly mattered?

Now we were indeed, housed in the Tower. Our apartment was not lavish, of course but clean and heated and the food was good. Margaret seemed not to know the passing of the days and nights. Whilst I, I waited in trepidation for Richard, My Lord of Gloucester.

I kept repeating to myself that he was no longer my childhood friend. He was a man who had fought with his brother and King, and won. I was the widow of their enemy. Would I be incarcerated into a nunnery? I knew I could expect no better.

It was a summer evening when he came. We had walked in the gardens and just come indoors for refreshments, when I was summoned. "My Lord of Gloucester waits for your attendance, My Lady." The man led me through the passageways to a plush solar. 'This must be the royal apartment.' The thought startled me, why had Richard, My Lord of Gloucester sent for me to come here?

I would know soon enough. As I entered the room, he turned from the window. My heart somersaulted as I curtsied low, waiting for his command to rise. But all he said was "Anne?" I raised my head, wondering, as he came over to reach down with his hands to lift me to my feet. "Still in mourning My Lady?" he queried gently, as he viewed the wimple. I shook my head, wanting to say so much but afraid he would not understand.

"Margaret," I touched the sign of my widowhood, "Margaret made me, Richard." There, I had done it again. Using his name familiarly, instead of his title, which was all I was now due. But he did not seem to mind. Just nodded and led me to a window seat.

"Tell me," he spoke softly and gravely; and so I did. It all came pouring out like a torrent of water breaking through a dammed river.

As I ran out of words he lifted my hand with its wedding ring still on my finger. He did not speak, just raised his eyebrow, as Edward had done.

"How could I take it off?" I said to him, "just like the wimple, it is all she has left of him, her son." He nodded and then said, "well Anne, the King has asked me to do what I will with you and I have only one question before I decide." I waited hardly breathing, and he took my hands in his and said, "do you love me Anne?" It was not the question I had expected and my face must have shown this. "Come," he said, "let us walk in the garden." And walk we did and we talked also. Recapturing old memories, remembering our dreams.

So that when he asked again, I could say with truth and certainty, "Yes Richard, yes, I love you. I think that I always have loved you and that, no matter what, I always will." He touched my cheek gently, "and I you Anne, and I you."

We smiled at one another and then he had to go to see the King at Westminster. "I will be back," he promised "soon."

His interview with Ned must have gone well, for he returned next day to take me out of my prison, to reside at Westminster. George, however, insisted that, until I was married, I was vulnerable and should stay at the Herber with my sister Isabel and himself as my only family.

He opposed my marriage to Richard fearing to lose all of the lands that he had been granted after father's death. Richard and he argued bitterly, George preferring me to go into a nunnery than be married to his brother. I was equal heir to my father's lands, with Isabel, but father had died a traitor and all had changed. Ned did not seem to remember that George too had plotted against him, turning coat at the last moment to secure himself in his brother's favour.

Ned gave in to him, as Ned always seemed to give in to George. So I went to live at the Herber, and Richard came to visit every day. Our wedding plans going on apace, whilst we waited for the Popes dispensation, as we were cousins and for George and Richard to reach an agreement on which of my father's lands I, and therefore Richard, was entitled to. Edward sent Richard north to keep the peace and the borders. Nothing could spoil my joy, the hated wimple was gone and the wedding band and I was simply Lady Anne Neville, once more.

It was lovely being with Isabel again. Now that I too had lost my chance of wearing the crown all her anger dissipated. We were sisters and she had her first born, named for his King, to coo over and care for. Edward, by allowing her husband my father's lands south of the Trent and the marcher lands, had left them wealthy. I of course had nothing. My father was attainted with treason and this meant that his lands were forfeit to the crown to dispose of as Ned wished.

Richard had been given Middleham, Sherriff Hutton and Penrith Castles and land and George all the Neville land and castles south of the Trent. This was of course, what they now argued about; Richard felt that the rest of my father's lands should now come back to me and through me to him, now I was respectable again and soon to be a Plantagenet. George, always jealous, not satisfied with his vast lands and the wealth that went with them, hated his little brother getting anything. It probably rankled that Richard had earnt the rewards his brother had given him by his loyalty and his skill in battle. George had his fortune due to Isabel being a Neville and his brother's extreme generosity to him.

Ned was not foolish, he knew whom he could trust to hold the North for him and keep the borders safe. He trusted Richard and had agreed to our marriage once Margaret had confirmed that her son and I had always slept apart. Richard told me of their interview with her. She had drawn herself up and almost spat out her distrust of Warwick and her determination that her son would beget no Neville brood.

'No they had not been bedded, nor were going to be. Of course Warwick had not known this. He had thought to see his daughter on the throne. It was laughable really; the great Warwick so easily duped, made blind by his ambition.

Once the throne was won Edward would have divorced Anne for not bearing children. Everyone would have accepted this, it happened in aristocratic families. Then her boy would have married someone worthy of him!' Her voice had broken, realising, suddenly that all this was in the past. Richard watched my face as he recounted the episode. Stroking my cheek occasionally.

I knew he expected me to be hurt by Margaret's revelation but it was what I had expected and part of me was glad that, either way, I would never have been truly Edward's wife. How they planned to do all this, had my father lived was not revealed and Ned and Richard did not ask. No doubt they planned his early demise I thought. As it was, after all his battles for York, he had lost his life fighting for Lancaster. Johnny too was dead and Richard and I planned to ask Ned for the ward-ship of his son, George.

I agreed, of course we must have him with us at Middleham. As well as Richard's two bastard children, Richard and Kathryn, we would fill Middleham with the laughter of children. I, who had always been protected, had found out suddenly what it was like to be friendless and alone. In my 16th year I vowed that no child would be made to feel unloved if myself, or Richard, could do anything to prevent it. Richard had agreed laughing gently at what he called my soft heart and hugging me close for agreeing to mother his two, bastard children. How could I refuse after my experience at the hands of greed and ambition, my father's and George's? They were children, innocent and I would raise them with my own.

My mother too, would live with us, Richard promised. He thought Ned's decree to be harsh; many of my father's lands had been her inheritance, brought to my father through her link to the Despensers but Warwick was dead and beyond punishment, what else could Ned do but punish her?

If he would but grant that my mother could live, with us, at Middleham, she would be happy enough and grateful not to have to end her days in Beaulieu Abbey, no matter how kind the nuns were. I had written, telling her the news of my impending marriage, and how we hoped once married, that the King would listen to Richard's petition, to allow her to come to Middleham. Richard's loyalty extended to all for whom he cared and my mother had been as a mother to him, in his time at Middleham, he would not forget.

Chapter 15

Beaulieu

I hated the Abbey. The confinement. The stone cells. Suddenly my life had been wrenched apart, for I was leaving the abbey to join Anne and Margaret when the news came to me of my husband's death in battle, at Barnet. Lord Scrope had sent a messenger to me as soon as they had heard that my ship had put into port. At first I wished that I too could die, or that my ship had foundered in the cold seas of the Channel. I then waited to hear how things fared for Lancaster, for with Lancaster was Anne. Isabel as George's wife was safe if Ned won or lost for George would simply turn coat again.

Anne however, had been married to the contender for Ned's throne, and I feared would be the loser even if Lancaster won. For I had first hand knowledge of Anjou's distrust of Warwick and I could not see her allowing a Neville on the throne, now my Lord was dead.

With my lord dead, Somerset would head the army of Lancaster, guiding the untried Edward through his first battle. Whatever the outcome, I could see no place for me. I would have to resign myself to Abbey life or, if allowed some of my land and Manors, to retire and live quietly. Anne would always have a place with me, I vowed, I had guessed Lancaster's intent not to consummate their marriage and turn her off as barren so he could wed another. With My Lord dead, Anne also had no one to protect her. If Lancaster lost, I could not think that Ned would deal harshly with a young girl, who had no say in her fate. We always said, I reminded myself; York does not make war on women and children.

In this I was right. Anne was to be married to Richard. Was I surprised? Part of me, yes, knowing he already had my lands he did not need to marry Anne, who had been, in truth joint heiress with her sister, Isobel. Then I remembered their friendship at Middleham and the beginnings of something deeper as they grew older. Yet Richard and Anne had not met for some years, could it be he loved her still and she him? Then came her letter, explaining all, and promising all would be well. Richard had promised they would see me at Middleham.

Meanwhile, I had my clothes and goods that had gone with me to France. I would do well enough. But it helped to know that both my girls would be safe, if only George did not cause too much trouble or change Ned's mind.

Why did Ned heed his brother so? I wondered. Maybe for Edmund's sake, they had been so close. Edmund, however, had been loyal, like Richard, but George, I shook my head, who knew with George?

They married quietly in St. Stephen's Chapel, Westminster. With Ned and his mother present and also Isobel. George had refused to attend, but Cecily, God bless her, had ensured that Isobel could see her sister wed. I wished that I could have been there, but Ned was still angry with my dead Lord, and who could blame him?

I would bide my time and pray that Richard's petition to his brother, for my release into his care, would be granted.

Saint George's Day 1472

I looked at the bundle in my arms. He lay quietly gazing up at me. So small I was almost afraid to touch him in case I was too rough. After my despair at my father's death and my ill treatment by George, I thanked God daily for bringing me to my safe haven of Middleham and Richard.

Our son was born, safely delivered and Richard had permission from his brother to bring my mother out of Beaulieu Abbey to abide with us at Middleham.

His nurse, Isabel came in to put him in his cradle.

I kept him nearby to me, not wanting to lose him to his nurses and the nursery. The time would come but not yet, he was still so new and small. Ladies did not feed their babies and Richard found a wet nurse, from the village, Ann Idley. I insisted on feeding him at first but I had little milk and he was so hungry and so I handed him over, reluctantly, to Isabel. The nursery was nearby so that I could be with him.

His nurses where loving and kind and I could trust them but he was my son and Richard's and I did not want to miss a minute of this miracle, given by God. I wanted to watch him change and grow. To see him crawling and watch his first steps and teach him. So my mother found us when, at last she arrived.

Bolton Castle

We drove across the dales from Middleham. This time we were staying in Middleham to take part in the festival, no longer were we just visitors or tourists, but part of what was happening in the town. More importantly to us both, we were part of honouring the memory of Richard III. We had never been to Bolton Castle on our trips north, to Sherriff Hutton yes, but not to Bolton. If you look at Bolton Castle, we were told, you will see that Sherriff Hutton was built on the same lines. Possibly by the same architect and builders.

It was a rainy day, and we had Pepi dog with us. It rained a lot in the Dales and one does not visit the area if one is going to be put off by a little rain. For me it was beautiful in any weather, the sun of course shows the countryside of at its best, but the rain brings out the mystic element of the region.

We arrived in the car park and picnic area, which we used, feeding the crows and taking Pepi for a walk so that she would enjoy a rest in the car, whilst we looked round the castle. Vineyards were growing in a walled garden, and a medieval garden had been planted. The view stretched to the woods and all the land belonged to the castle. I began to see, in my mind's eye, how the grounds of Sherriff Hutton too might have looked. Up the steps we went to the castle only to find we had gone the wrong way and had to be re-directed, by a nice lady in the shop. So we began our exploration, of kitchens and of course the brewhouse, without which no respectable castle could be thought worthy. No wonder Richard had had so many added to his castles I chortled.

There were stables where horses would have been kept, the courtyard, still showing marks where pig and sheep pens would have housed livestock. The armourer, though it looked a dark old place for doing any skilled work. The chapel with a room off to the side, called a Solar but I doubted that, I felt it was more probable that this was used for the women to hear the service when the weather was cold, for there was a fireplace, and the room was small. It gave us an idea of how the chapel at Middleham might have looked, however. We stood up high on one of the Tower's and took photo's across the battlements and the crows, who were, no doubt, the descendants of those crows that the owners of Bolton had put on their family crest, and flag, a flag, which flew proudly from the castle even now.

On we went entering the upper floors where there was also a kitchen and dining hall, bedrooms and a main room with a huge fireplace and small oven at the side. The nursery led off from this main room and though I was not convinced that the older children portrayed would have slept so near to the Solar. I wondered if a young one may have been so slept, so that a new baby and maybe a new mother would not be parted?

Chapter 16
Treason

The tension showed not only in his body and the lines etched suddenly upon his face, but in his eyes. The sorrow, not for one lost brother, but for two. For Richard knew that as surely as he was losing George to the charge of treason, so he was also losing Edward – Ned – the brother he worshipped.

As often as I had wished for Richard not to see Edward with such blinding love – I was loath to see the realisation, the thought that, his golden brother – his Lord – his King – was only of gilt and that much tarnished. In truth Edward was just a man and could not have hoped to live up to the pedestal on which Richard had placed him when he (Richard) was Dickon and an adoring youngest brother.

Suddenly my own thoughts drifted back to happier times, when my father was Lord of Warwick Castle, and the four of us, Isabel, George, Richard and I were children. I had not been frightened of George then – as I had learned to be later – after my father had lured him into many treasonable actions, including marriage to my sister – expressly forbidden by the King, his brother – Edward – Ned.

What was it about George, I wondered, he seemed to change from a sunny, laughing, loveable lad to a person who inspired not loyalty but fear. He could be so nice, pleasant, charming but he could, as suddenly, change – why? What was it that made this happen?

"Schizophrenia." A voice spoke – I looked up from the book I was reading – but I had not been spoken to. Two sixth form girls sitting opposite me, in the Library's reading room, where looking up words in a dictionary, and one girl had spoken, loudly. "Sch, Sch, Sch" a few readers shook their heads disapprovingly.

*　　　　*　　　　*　　　　*　　　　*

The messenger had arrived from Edward as Richard had returned from a routine border patrol. He like to ride the Northern border and it heartened his men to see him at the mundane times of the on going task of keeping the border peaceful. Sometimes there may be skirmishes to turn back Scots raiders and to prevent them disturbing the peace of the border villages.

Other wise the border patrol was fairly uneventful. Official raids into Scotland to keep the King's Peace had become rare. Edward preferred to negotiate than waste money on battles. He had seen the ongoing battles of his youth drain England's resources and her stability. He was determined that his reign would bring England trade and thereby wealth, not to be frittered away needlessly. The damage in the 'hundred years war', culminating in England's losses in France of all her territory, apart from Calais, had lost the English any desire for battle. What did they gain in the end except death and disease?

Now George, apparently bored with soft living; now that my father was no longer around, to drag him off into impossible battles, had seemingly thrown down the gauntlet once too often to his brother and King. That was George's problem, I thought, he saw Ned as just Ned, never as his King. He hated the Wydvilles, never ceasing to slur the Queen and her kin, in his brother's presence and to any who might listen.

I may not live at Court but Richard had been to his nephew's wedding and he thought that his pleas had worked but I had letters telling me the news and Isobel wrote of her fear that George's treasonable talk would push Edward's patience too far. She had been glad of her pregnancy as an excuse to leave the Herber and stay at their manor in Tewkesbury, to have her baby. Antoinette, our one time nurse, had helped the Queen through her latest confinement and Isobel had asked her be in attendance at her own. Antoinette lived in Somerset now and as the Queen had also added her pleas to my sisters, she could not refuse.

Now Isobel was dead. A few months after the birth, both she and the boy, Richard had succumbed to a hacking cough, bringing up blood and unable to breathe. George had seemed demented. He had ranted and raved and sent his private army to pull Antoinette from her bed and accused her of poisoning his wife and child. It was not true of course and he had no proof or reason to suspect. But the Queen had been instrumental in Antoinette's being at the birth and that was enough for George. He had accused our dear, good, now old, nurse and had had her put to death.

There was outrage, of course through out the country and for once both the King and Queen were in agreement, this could not be allowed to lie. Only the King had the power to try and sentence someone, and Antoinette was known and liked by the royal family as she was to us. She had but recently helped the Queen in childbed, before attending Isobel; the implications in George's actions were plain.

What had pushed George to such a treasonable act? Surely Edward denying him the right to become one of the suitors to Mary of Burgundy was not the cause? Even George must realise, surely, that Edward could not risk allowing his brother to become head of a country like Burgundy even had his loyalty not been questionable, it was too soon, I felt, after Isobel's death. I admit I did not understand Edward's allowing his brother-in-law to become one of Mary's suitors, but I was not sure of the Wydville's loyalty, anymore than George's.

The games played at Court, vying for power and position, made them all questionable in my view. George of course, had thrown a tantrum in the Council chamber, but Mary was not foolish it seemed, and Maximillian it was who won her hand and Burgundy. The rift that it caused between George and Ned was irreparable, it seemed.

Now an innocent woman had paid for George's treason, with her life. Now Ned had to act, and, being Ned once the decision was made, justice followed swiftly. George was arrested and tried on the charge of treason, and Ned had been his sole accuser and witness against his brother. Surely this was not just about George's murder of Antoinette? He had put up with worse from George, over the years.

George, who had taken up arms against his brother and been forgiven so many times had now acted and been unable to be forgiven.

What else, I wondered had he done to tip the balance in the Wydvilles's favour for Edward to agree that the only course left was to condemn his own brother for treason?

"I must stop him." Richard said. "I know what George has done but Ned must not kill him – he will never forgive himself nor live well with this on his conscience." Ned was not as soft as Richard. He only killed for a reason but once a decision was made he kept to it and he bore it like the King he, in truth was, believing right to be on his side. He had often chided Richard for what he termed lovingly as Richard's 'damned conscience'. Especially when Richard presumed to take him to task or question his decisions.

Richard stood re-reading his brother's missive after the messenger had gone to eat and rest. There would be no return message, for Richard would go himself to plead, not just for his one brother's life but for the other brother's soul.

I watched as the disbelief showed again in Richard's face, this was Ned! Ned for whom the family held the strongest tie. Surely there was nothing worse than that which George had already done, pitting himself time and again against his brother and his King. Why did Edward break at this time, a time of peace, to yell treason at his brother and allow the sentence of death?

I shuddered as I held him, no words of mine could heal the rift George's death would bring betwixt Richard and Ned. If Richard could not persuade Ned to repeal his brother's sentence it would change everything between them.

*   *   *   *   *

We had come to Middleham, to see Geoffrey and to spend the bank holiday weekend taking slides, not just of Middleham Castle but had stopped at Pontefract on our journey up. We needed slides of Richmond too and were lucky that the sun had decided to shine for us. People who re-enacted how life was lived in the medieval period, where setting up their tents and stalls and fires as we walked round the castle.

We were pleased, the weekend looked as if it was going to be really interesting. Sunday at Middleham, and being actually in the castle grounds was always a pleasure but with the re-enactors showing how bows were made and used as well as swords, he was in his element.

We would never get the slides I needed and so I took the camera determined to take the shots I wanted myself. Eventually going up on to the platform along the battlements, to look over at the mound that was the first Castle, Williams mound.

Part Two
The Protector

Richard III

Chapter 1
Edward

It was my own special place, mine and Johnny's. Everyday when the weather was kind to us, we would escape from our lessons and books and make our way across the yard and out of the gateway. Through fields grown high with summer grass and with wild yellow flowers that my father and mother loved. For they made it look as if our Castle was surrounded by a yellow sea with waves rippling to the walls as the wind played amongst the yellow blooms, bending them this way and that.

Sheep now grazed in the old castle ruins and on the hill it stood upon and the sunshine pooled into bright patches. Which made the shade look dark and full of mystery. Ghosts of our Neville ancestors walked here, so my Nurse, Isabel would tell me but on a glorious warm spring or summer day I could only feel joy and ease in the old ruins, these ruins that had once been the Neville's pride and joy before our newer castle of Middleham had been built. This lay below us as we climbed the old battlements and towers. The hustle and bustle lost behind its magnificent walls which seemed so strong, so permanent that they would last forever. "Naught lasts forever." 'Johnny' (he hated his given name, George and so we called him, as he wished, after his father) would say, looking both sad and wise. For John had lost father and uncle both, in rebellion against the King; a King who was mine own father's brother and my uncle. John, Marquis of Montague had been 'Johnny's' father and a loyal Yorkist until his brothers uprising against the King. He had been found dead, wearing the emblem of York beneath his Neville breastplate.

"Why?" I asked my father once, when he had returned weary from one of the border skirmishes against the Scots. "Why did 'Johnny's' father rebel against Uncle Edward? He who was always loyal?"

My father had replied to me gravely, as man to man, as to the future Lord of Middleham. "My Lord of Montague was also mine own Uncle and loyal to Edward my brother and King. Before Edward and I were chased out of England by my Uncle of Warwick, Montague had been dispossessed of his title of Northumberland, a title taken from the Percies and now given back to them by Edward.

He thought to command their loyalty by returning their title and lands. John was given the title of Montague and made a Marquis and recompensed for his loss but John had always been loyal to Edward and had fought for his King no matter what, even against his own brother. As Earl of Northumberland he would have held against his brother, Warwick as he had always done. Edward's actions seemed to John a betrayal of his loyalty and whilst we were in Burgundy he joined his brother's cause.

Being the man he was, once given to his brother, his loyalty remained true, even to fighting against those he loved. So he had fought for Edward against Warwick. So now he fought for Warwick against Edward. It was a waste Edward." He spoke to me but his eyes were distant as if re-living a conversation with the King. He looked back at me. "Yet when we landed at Ravenspur, with few rallying to our cause, John let us march south and did not attack us, as he surely could have. And Percy sat in his Northumberland stronghold refusing to support his King despite his regained title.

"But you won." I whispered.

"Ay Edward, we won but at what cost? The Wydvilles reign supreme at Court, with none to gainsay them. They owe their allegiance to the King but to the house of York? No, to the House of York they owe the deaths and ridicule of their husbands and sons. I do not believe," he regarded m soberly, "that they will ever forgive York for these actions. Only the King stops their allegiance to Lancaster, if we had not the King what then?" he grimaced, "it does not bear thinking about."

"Is it true?" I asked, "that Uncle John wore his York halberd under his armour?"

"Ay lad," my father's arm was round my shoulders, "ay, he remained at heart, for York. I wept to seem him laid low, next to his brother at Westminster. With his child dispossessed and his wife homeless, for this one, foolish though treasonable, act."

"Is this why 'Johnny' lives here, with us?" I ventured.

"Ay, and we wanted your cousin Edward too, as you know. He may be simple but your mother's care would have cherished him." He did not add, although I knew that the Queen's son, Dorset had been granted the ward-ship of Uncle George's son, I prayed that his wife would care for my cousin as my mother would have, had he come to Middleham.

My Uncle Edward, I knew had since returned Uncle John's lands to his widow, through my own father's intercession with the King. Grandmother

Neville too had been released into my parent's care here at Middleham, and she had arrived soon after my birth. But my father could not get his brother to budge over the care of Cousin Edward and soon no doubt it would be time for him to be presented at court.

I wondered if I would ever go to Court with my father, who hated the times when he had to go and leave my mother and me. Yet he cherished his brother, I knew, and the times he had to spend on his own with the King. His was the only advice my uncle would listen to and sometimes take, other than the Wydvilles. "They think me boorish and stupid," my father confided to me, "a country clod, it is for the best." He looked at me once more eye to eye. "Never let your enemy know your strength Edward, never let them have the measure of you. Then you will always have the element of surprise on your own side and God only knows when one will need it."

I nodded gravely. My father spoke from years of experience of keeping the borders safe from the Scots of battles and of diplomacy. His words were to be remembered and cherished, to be used when I joined him, fighting by his side and learning the craft of war in battle, as one could only, to then, put the skills learnt in the tiltyard, into practice.

We talked about it,' Johnny' and I, as we practised in the Castle ruins, with wooden swords and shields. Planning the destruction of the Scots and pretending to lay siege and conquer the ruins of the old castle. The stone that had not been used in the building of Middleham's new castle, still standing in the walls and towers, most of the internal stone had been taken and re-used when the new castle was built. My father had also had alterations done to the castle, as other owners before him. Putting in large windows too which let in more light, as well as wooden walkways from turret to turret, across the courtyard. So now one could walk without the gales tearing off our cloaks or the sleet or snow soaking us through. Our guests, and we always had some visitors, the ladies most especially, were most thankful for this innovation. Which meant that heavy winter skirts did not get heavy with mud or water and slippers did not have to be shoved into patens.

The men too, if truth be told, preferred also to preserve their new doublets and hose and woollen cloaks, as well as their moulded leather boots or shoon. The central hall and the rooms above were also linked to the guest quarters and the upper rooms of the castle by the same, albeit smaller, wooden walkways.

They all sported glass windows to look out at the weather, rain or shine and to let the light in.

Mine own tower was therefore now linked, not just by the stone passageways but also by the wooden bridges. Not just my tower, but shared with my cousin 'John', it had also housed my elder brother, also a John and my father's bastard whom he had brought to Middleham with his sister Kathryn to be cared for and brought up with us. Both had been my dear companions and family since my birth. John was grown up now and Kathryn's companions were other girls of good birth. I rejoiced that 'Johnny' and I still had the freedom to play and to tell each other stories in the security of our tower bedroom. In winter a fire was kept burning low all night and we fell asleep to the crackling of the burning logs and flames dancing patterns across the painted walls.

My mother eschewed battle scenes for our bedroom. Horses seemed to dance and gallop round the room, bearing ladies and gentlemen with their hawks. The thick arras that covered our window was broidered with bright birds flying into the sun; the rose en soleil, of course; away from the falcons which, further round the wall, hunted and sometimes caught their prey.

*   *   *   *   *

A whole week at Middleham this was my idea of heaven. Geoffrey would be up at the weekend and meanwhile we had a week to explore the surrounds and to contact people in the town who had now become friends.

We left at five in the morning, loaded up as usual and Pepi dog in the back. The cottage was one we usually hired in Back Street, near to the castle and far away enough not to be bothered by tourists. The sun shone and we made good time. I was to give a talk and slide show but instead of being involved daily in the celebrations for Richard and Anne's coronation week, as I had done previously, I was only one part of the whole. This time not running a stall, or looking for information. This week we could relax and enjoy the area. It was exciting to be part of an event that had become so big and we hoped the weather would hold.

The castle, as ever, seemed like coming home, and Maureen was there to greet us and so was Keith. I did my normal splurge on books, whilst he groaned 'not more books, we don't have the room.' There would be medieval tents and stalls again at the weekend but for now it was just itself, with Richard's statue now looking part of the whole, as it weathered.

I wondered what it had really been like 550 years ago. When Richard had been born and when he owned the castle. When news of Edward's death had been brought to Richard and Anne, knowing the changes this news brought. the changes in their life together but not realising just how deep those changes would be. Their son Edward too, how would he have felt, how affected by this sudden and unexpected change to his life?

He was not quite eleven years of age when it all happened. Did he give thought to his Cousin, now King but also having to deal with the loss of his father? Was he excited at the prospect that he might go to London, as his father was now Protector? Or was he scared, if it was frightening for Anne and Richard, how might he, a boy, have felt?

I wondered too if Earl Rivers had set out later than his sister anticipated, when he began the journey with the new King, to London, to give Edward time to mourn his father. How had Middleham mourned? Or was the death of the King, so far away, in London, only real because it meant that their own Lord was to leave them, and who knew for how long? Oh to be able to look back and see!

     *   *   *   *   *

My mother never failed to come and see us on her way round the castle, doing the checks for security that my father did when he was home. Then they did them together, both creeping in to see if we slept. If awake, we were chided and then hugged.

If we slept my mother smoothed our brows with her hands and kissed our foreheads, my father watching from the foot of our bed, smiling at the pleasant picture we made. My nurses Isabel and Ann told us of their nightly visits.

As I grew older, although Isabel and Jane stayed, pages began to take their place and gentlemen of the bedchamber and Hugh who guided our prowess at tiltyard and butts. My mother still saw to our education in letters, law, reading, music and etiquette just as her mother, Grandma Neville had taught my own mother and her sister as well as my father. She told us our history, the Neville's and the Plantagenet's, and when she spoke of my father her voice was a caress.

I was ten years of age when our world was turned upside down. We had seen the single horseman clatter over the drawbridge. Dusty from the road he fell into the courtyard as men rushed to help him and take his horse, 'John' and I with them. The man knelt, exhausted on the cobbles, "My Lord of Gloucester." He barely breathed the words and as a page prepared to fetch my father I stepped forward. "Wait," I said, "see who he's from." Security had ever to be maintained, it was imprinted in me, do not act from emotion or impulse, check first. This was my father's tenet and Hugh's, my teacher. The man held papers stating his name and his master, William, Lord Hastings, the King's dearest friend. He was divested of sword and dagger and I led him up to the Great Hall. As we entered my father descended the stairs, my mother close behind. The aura of urgency and disaster that surrounded the man, as he rode into the castle, seemed to imbue the whole castle and us with dread.

"My Lord," the man walked towards my father and knelt as my father descended the stairs and approached him.

"Father," I said, "this man rides in haste. He has a letter of passage from my Lord Hastings. He has been checked and his weapons removed."

My father smiled at me. "Well done, Edward. Now, he frowned at the messenger, "what, pray does My Lord Hastings have to say that it is so urgent and that my brother does not send to me?" The man withdrew a parchment from his doublet, holding it out to my father; his head forwards, down to his arm. His dark cloak fell open; he was dressed from head to foot in black.

In black! My face paled, why had we, none of us, noticed? My father noticed and my mother too. Their faces paled also and their eyes met as my father unscrolled the message. Blunt and brief as was Lord Hastings way, he informed my father, on behalf of the Council, that his brother, his Lord, his King, was dead. He had died a few weeks before my 10th birthday, a few days after Easter, and would be buried in St. George's Chapel, as he desired. The second parchment was held out.

This was from Hastings personally to my father. "My Lord" he read, "my friend and King your brother died on 9 April and was on 21 April, interred in St. George's' Chapel, Windsor. The Queen Dowager sends for her son, to Ludlow and the Coronation date is set for 4 May.

The King, my Lord, named you as Lord Protector until Edward comes of age and the Council has agreed to this. I bid you come to London in haste with a goodly amount of men. The King will be accompanied by my Lord Rivers, his household, plus 2,000 armed soldiers. May the holy trinity have you in their keeping." In haste, at Westminster, Hastings.

My father read, aloud, slowly, for the enormity of the news to sink in. The King, Uncle Edward, his beloved brother, dead, this could not be. He looked to question the man kneeling, faint and weary at his feet, then nodded. "Anne," and he held out his arm out to my mother. "Edward come." I obeyed, approaching him at speed. His hand dropped briefly to my head. "You heard?" I nodded. "Go, get George and join us in the Solar.

You," he beckoned a page, "see this man refreshed and bathed, find him fresh clothes, then bring him to us." He looked at the messenger, kindly but firm, "You have an hour, then we wish to know all you can tell us." As I left to find where 'Johnny' had got to I heard orders to get ready to depart, ringing out.

'John' was not hard to find, he had stayed in the doorway as the man had entered and offered his missives. He had heard the news as my father had read it out. Gravely 'John' took my hand and led me to our tower.

"You heard?" I gasped, unintentionally echoing my father's words to me. He nodded, "My father wishes us both with him and my mother." We walked into our tower and up to our room and up again to the turret top overlooking the moors and our old castle, now with cloaks pulled round us.

"Your father will be busy organising his departure," he said "let us wait an hour and go to him then." 'John' looked at me, "his brother has died," he said gently, "it is a load to bear." I nodded and then remembered.

He is to be Lord Protector, what does that mean?" 'John' frowned, a few years older and wiser than myself he remembered his history. "Lord Protector's are to guide the young King and his Council until they may rule by themselves. The King will be head of State but your father," 'John' looked solemn, "why Ned, he will have to help your cousin rule England."

His voice was hushed in awe, but I? I only saw that my father was leaving not to visit London, but to stay. Would my mother go with him? And I? Where would I fit into all this? I looked into 'John's' dark blue eyes, "I am afraid," I whispered softly, ashamed of my fear and my selfish thoughts. But 'John' seemed to understand, as he always did. He gave me a bear hug.

"No need for that – come." He gave me his hand and hoisted me up as we heard Hugh calling us. My father's summons had come.

*   *   *   *   *

Chapter 2
Protector of the Realm

16 April 1483

I watched Richard's face as he scanned the missives from Hastings and the King's Council and the second, from Hastings alone. We had both known, from the messengers black clothes, why the message came from Hastings and not the King. The King was dead. Laughing, hugely alive, bright as the sun, all those Edward had been and now he was no more. A light had gone out of Richard's world and his eyes were dark ringed as if he'd had the worst of a fight. Yet he gave his orders, coolly and simply.

He would travel to York, he told me and have a Mass said for Edward's soul. He sent out messengers to all the Northern Lords to meet him at York and declare their allegiance to the new King, Edward V. He wrote at once to Lord Rivers, begging his reply to be sent to him at York, so that they may arrange to meet on the road and bring the King to London and his coronation together. He did not mention that by ordering the King to London and naming his coronation day the dowager-queen was, in fact, acting treasonably. Only the appointed Lord Protector could do these things.

He knew that I was worried, "they will seek to entrap you, my love. Do as Hasting's advises and take two thousand men with you." He smiled at my concern, "Nay my love, then I would be the aggressor and Sir Anthony could claim his force to be but to match mine. Do not worry, I am aware." A knock on the solar door and Hugh was admitted. "My Lord," he bowed, "as I left to call the boys a man came up from London." Richard raised an eyebrow, "another Hugh?" he smiled.

"My Lord, he is from the Duke of Bockenham, he will give none his message but you. He is clean of weapons, my lord, shall I bring him to you, or?" He left the query hanging in the air. "Ay Hugh, then fetch the boys", he laughed at Hugh's look of concern. "Do not worry Hugh, Harre of Bockenham has no gripe with me." I moved and sat a little aside as this new messenger arrived. "My Lord." The man dropped to one knee and held out a parchment, Richard read, then handed it to me. It was headed Richard, Lord Protector of England, and read "My Lord, I grete you well. I have great sorrow to inform you of your brother's death as I know of none who has so informed you. I pledge myself and as many men as you may wish, to come to you anywhere you may desire of me. For the weal and fortune of England. May the holy trinity have you in their keeping. Harre Bockenham."

"Is there aught else?" Richard asked. "My Lord," the man spoke, "my master begs you come with all speed. For, he says to tell you that the Wydville woman will take the King into her keeping and through his crown rule the countrie. The Council support her, My Lord, except my own Lord and Hastings. "Thank you," Richard answered, "now go, refresh yourself and tomorrow I would have you return to my cousin with a letter," the man nodded, bowed, and left.

"I told you Richard," I said, "That there was a trap."

"Ay love, but its not sprung yet and with Bockenham's help and the Lord, we may yet get the better of them," he frowned, "I wish a service for Edward's soul and a te dium at the church. Our people of Middleham must be told of the King's death and to be allowed to grieve."

"And you Richard?" I laid my hand on his arm "when will you grieve?" He smiled with his mouth but his eyes were dark and hurt, "I? I will grieve my love, for ever."

*　　　　　*　　　　　*　　　　　*　　　　　*

'My dearest Anne, my love, I grete you well and beg you will attend myself and the King, in London. As you see I stay at our good friend's house, John Paston, and miss your presence. No need to bring 'our boy', as we agreed, London being no place to bring him if not necessary. I enclose details of my journey to London, which as you will see was quite eventful. I hope Edward, my nephew, will come to understand my reasons, and not hate me too much. He has, unfortunately, been brought up a Wydville, which my one time good friend Thomas Vaughan has done nothing to alleviate, being now in their camp. You will understand all from the enclosed. Be assured of my love and kindness to you and our son, always. Bid Hugh look after you both well, from your good lord and husband, Richard.'

The Journey

The masses were sung at York Cathedral and the Lords came to answer my summons. I knelt at the High altar, pledging Edward V as my Liege Lord and requiring all the Noble Lords to do the same. It had been a week and the reply had come from Ludlow. Earl Rivers would bring the King to Northampton to intercept our journey from York. There the King and Lord Protector would meet journey together to London. I had 500 gentlemen with me and had bade Buckingham meet me with an hundred more. If my plan went well 600 men would be plenty.

The King was not at Northampton when we arrived, Earl Rivers alone met me. There were plainly not enough rooms to house my men and the King's, so he explained. The King was waiting at Stony Stratford; I could join him on the morrow.

'Ay', I thought, 'and am I to be ambushed on the road as I ride to meet my nephew?' Harre of Bockenham was there to meet me before River's had arrived, and we had planned an ambush of our own.

That River's had come with a few retainers was un-looked for luck. We could keep him at our inn, with no need now, to worry about surrounding the inn at Stony Stratford and frightening Edward. With Rivers in our snare the rest should come quietly and the soldiers, a long way from Wales would, we hoped, go gratefully home.

I had received a second missive from Hastings, begging me to hasten to London with an army to defeat the Wydville attempt to rule via the Protectorship and then the Crown through the boy King. I smiled. I would need no army, only to be up a lot earlier than my enemies. With Rivers trapped in the inn and his people waiting at Stony Stratford for his early return, to signal their treason, I would have them caught in my trap, instead of I in theirs.

It was unfortunate that Edward would have to waken to my gentlemen taking over from his Ludlow household. His men would be dismissed back to Ludlow and the soldiers back to Wales. Edward had been in Ludlow 11 years. Learning his books and how to manage his household. My brother had thought it best but as you well know, I had never understood how he or Elizabeth could be apart from their son and at such a young age though I was part of Edward's council and had helped choose the men who would tutor him. Thomas Vaughan an old retainer of the House of York had been my choice.

Yet he too had been seduced by the Wydville charm. He, with Lord Anthony and her son Richard Grey, had accompanied Edward to Stony Stratford with the purpose of ambushing and killing me, their two thousand soldiers against my 500 men and Harri's 100, should have been enough for their purpose.

Fortunately they had under estimated Richard of Gloucester. The country bumpkin, the clodhopper, the 'manner less fool', as she had once called me. Soon they will realise that one does not win battles by being a fool.

Edward was puzzled, of course, and afraid I think. He knows me only slightly, for his Uncle Rivers has been his mentor and guide for five years. With no other influence at Ludlow, Edward has been moulded into a Wydville. Clever, urbane, a poet and writer (Caxton has even printed one of his books), Anthony, Earl Rivers who is master at the tournai and brave in battle, is the stuff young men look to as their hero, much as I did to your father, in my youth. Anthony is a bit like Edward, I realise, my beautiful, clever, courageous but oft times foolish, brother. Understood his need to break your father's hold, but to replace it with the Wydvilles, instead of balancing the power amongst his council, this I did not understand. The Wydvilles so fair to look on but greedy, lusting after, and gaining power during my brother's reign, a power they are now so afraid of losing.

How could I explain this to Edward? My nephew knows less of the Court intrigues than I. Yet he has been well educated and is courteous, he has managed his household well under the guidance of Rivers and he is brave.

We had left Northampton at cockcrow but Edward was already upon his horse, with his household, when we arrived. Earl Rivers had planned well. I dismounted and bowed to our young King, Harre at my shoulder.

"My Liege," I said to him, "I have pledged my loyalty to you in York Minster, as did all your Northern Lords. My brother, your father, made me Lord Protector of your realm with the Council's agreement. Therefore, have I hastened to meet your Majesty, to accompany you to London. Edward answered me right bravely; "Thank you Uncle," he said, "but we are awaiting my Lord Rivers to join us."

Expecting this I tried to explain that a plot had been discovered against my life. That I was bound, as Lord Protector, to apprehend those guilty of this treasonable plotting and to replace his household and troops, for mine and his security, with those I could trust.

Only a boy, I thought, not yet twelve years of age, not much older than our own Edward. How could his mother and guardian's put him in to such a situation, all to gain the power to rule through a boy King.

As the changes to his household had to be made, I determined to take him back to Northampton to give him time to adjust and to try and explain. Earl Rivers was his mentor and his hero, whom he trusted. My words of treason and power must have seemed alien to him. Thomas Vaughan, my own choice, had been party to the Wydville plotting and that hurt most of all. How could Thomas be taken in? How could he believe that killing the Lord Protector was right? To go against Edward's final wish? Or had those wishes been dismissed as the foolish whim of a dying man? Previously the Queen dowager had been left as protector to the realm and their son. But then Edward was in France, expected to return. From death he knew there was no return and none knew the Wydvilles better than he, their greed, their frightening ambition and lust for power.

His son would be used ruthlessly he knew, as Henry VI had been, and England would again be drained of her riches. All Edward's hard work, building up trade and the royal treasury would be lost. Who else could he trust to uphold his law but myself; whose loyalty had been given, ay even when we disagreed, as you well know; all my life? How to explain all this to the boy who is also my Liege Lord and my King?

I did try, Anne. Talking gently I swear I was so careful but it must have seemed as if his world was turning upside down, again. "And my mother?" he asked me, "will she be in London?" How did I know what the Wydville woman had planned, or would do? However, I answered in hopes that her maternal instincts would play some role in all this. "Ay, my Liege and your brother and sisters too no doubt." He seemed reassured at this and I added, "believe me Edward, I have no more liking for all this than you." We talked then about his life at Ludlow and I of Middleham and of my own Edward. He asked if his cousin would visit London and be at his Coronation, and so we are commanded, my love, to let Edward come to London, but not yet.

If you mislike the thought we can always say he is too frail, no one knows him, so this will be readily accepted I think. They could meet on Edward's first progress, perhaps; maybe he will go to York or Durham, as his father used, it would be natural for him to visit the places my brother knew well.

We did talk of this and I told him of the rugged splendour of the north, the awesome waterfalls in full flood and the mountains towering over the land, the deep mists and glorious sunshine.

He asked about the battles I had fought with the Scots and I told him how I had held the borders for his father, and would for him if he so desired. We spoke of the skirmishes and the battles and how his father and I had fought side by side. In this wise did we spend our first evening and the many evenings on our way to London. I have also been trying to involve him in the decisions that needed to be made in the running of his realm.

A train of mules carried the armour and weapons that Earl Rivers had equipped his soldiers with. They preceded us to London, as proof to the Council and the citizens, of the Wydvilles attempt to rule through the young King after ambushing, and possibly killing, me. The Council already knew of course, for they are all Wydville men, all except Harre and William. Exposing the plot to the villages we passed through and to the Londoners themselves, meant that the Council had to decide to either give me their support to us, or the Dowager Queen. With all London aware of the plot and being loyal to Edward and now his son the Council had to uphold my brother's dying wish, they confirmed me as Lord Protector, until Edward comes of age.

I, in turn, have promised not to act alone but to be, in all wise, directed by the Council. But I jump ahead of events. We arrived in the City on May 4, the citizens cheered and the Lord Mayor met us with his Aldermen. Edward looked very fine in deep blue velvet. "We have made ready the Bishop's Palace my Liege, my Lord," he bowed to us both and I frowned, why? Why was it not Westminster? To his mama and sister's and young Richard? Edward needed to feel some normality around him. He would take on his kingly role soon enough.

I acquiesced, guessing a reason behind this good man's decision. Let the boy have a few more hours to be a boy, a brother, and a son. But I asked Harri to hi him to Westminster to see what was amiss. Meanwhile the King was ensconced in the Bishops' Palace and I sent my squire to see if I could, once more use Crosby Place.

Edward needs his own space, his own court, I am his advisor, head of the Council, but he is the King. Besides, once he is of an age to rule alone and make his own decisions with out need of guidance, I wish to return to Middleham to hold the North for my new King as I had for his father, God willing. This I have told him, I will be in London for as long as he needs me, but my wish is to return home. Once he feels able to rule alone, I will, with his leave, return to mine own estates.

He is bright, Anne and clever and with the Wydville influence diminished I have high hopes that Edward V will make a fine King.

A final note on which, as you will see I must close and will despatch this straight to you. Harri returned from Westminster. The Dowager Queen is gone with furniture, bedding, hangings, children and the treasury. She abides in the Abbott's lodgings at Westminster Abbey claiming sanctuary (from whom? her own son?) and the royal apartments are in an uproar and stripped bare. Make haste to come to me my love, I feel that I will be in sore need of your comfort and counsel. Richard'

Given at Crosby Place, the first day after St. Monica's.

4 May 1483

Richard had gone to York to hold a mass for Edward, his brother and erstwhile King, and then he was moving on to London to meet up with his new King, our new King, and accompany his King and nephew, into the city.

My own Edward, though only ten years of age, seemed to be growing up before my eyes. His cousin although six years his senior, now taking a back seat, allowing Edward to take the lead. One day Edward would hold Middleham and the north, as his father now did, in tandem with the Percies. It would soon be time, I sighed to myself to find both boys a wife.

Richard would plead the return of the Montague estates to his nephew, which was held by us in trust. John's widow already had an income from them, for Richard would not see her suffer. We had taken George (Johnny as he preferred to be called} as ward to help her it saved her the expense of his education. "Who else," Richard said, "would take on the lad of a man attainted?" Besides his father had served Edward well 'twas only at the end that he had supported his brother, my father. We had wanted George's son too but he had been warded to Dorset, the Queen's eldest son, who gained a goodly sum from the deal of course. I wondered how the lad would fare under that man's dubious care.

I was in the garden that my mother had had planted, so long ago. Edward had given her permission to live at Raby, a few years after she had come to live with us.

"I'll not have folk think she needs must hide from me behind my brother's coat." He told Richard, "besides, there are so many of you at Middleham - children everywhere - and worse when you have visitors. If your mother-in-law wishes to run her own establishment she may. Tell her I will return Raby to her."

She had accepted eagerly and I, though sorry to see her go, understood her need to be independent. Richard would allow her a portion of the revenues from the Warwick estate that he had been given on his brother's death. She would do well enough and we could visit one another, often, she told me.

The sun was warm and had been since April but a cold wind kept a cloak round my shoulders. Edward had been fooled by the warm weather, we had been told, had gone out in a boat, fishing, in just his shirtsleeves. The cold wind had given him a chill, a chill that killed him. A big man, like his legendary ancestor, Geoffrey Plantagenet, and like Geoffrey he was killed by a chill.

It did not seem possible, I mused, drinking in the smell of the early flowers. The daffodils had died but buds were appearing on the roses and heartsease and lavender and the hollyhock too were beginning to push themselves up out of the earth and the herbs were beginning to sprout.

Suddenly I saw Edward had come down from his rooms, he stood in the doorway of his tower. Foreboding gripped my heart as he ran towards me.

"Ma mere," he gasped, he was learning French I remembered. "Come quickly its 'Johnny,' he's not well. He looks greensick and has took to his bed."

I ran into the tower and up the winding stairs, for the first time regretting that we had not insisted the boys move into the more modern part of the castle.

I sat by the bed, which he shared with my son and felt his forehead, it was wet and sticky, all was clearly not well. Isobel hovered nearby and I sent her to get our good Doctor Pencryth, silently blessing Richard's insistence on keeping him as part of our household. He was soon with us, feeling my nephew's sticky brow, he then motioned to me and we left 'Johnny' with Isobel and Edward, who would not leave his side. "I do not know my lady," he answered my unspoken question, "it is a sweating sickness that could as easily depart as sudden as it came."

Sweating sickness, this time a real fear gripped me, in London people died of this, aye and in the country too, though less often. The person would get raging hot and with a thirst, 'twould peak into a fever and kill or cure the sufferer.

"I will do my best" the good Doctor assured me, "but as you know 'twill reach a fever and break and we will not be sure 'till then. He is young and strong," he carried on seeing my face, which must have drained of colour. "He has a good chance, pray my lady." He clasped my two hands in his own strong ones and went back up the stairs to 'Johnny'.

I went into the garden and stared helplessly round; sitting on an arbour bench I felt the tears welling up in my eyes. Angrily I brushed them away, no need to cry, he was a fighter, and strong as the Doctor said. I would pray but first I would have the kitchen brew an herb tea for 'Johnny'.

Gradually through the day he worsened, pushing his covers away, whilst we tried to keep him covered and warm. Isobel tried to get him to take the herb tea but though hot and dry he seemed unable to do more than sip it. I disregarded the Doctor eventually and opened a shutter to let the light in and I saw his eyes wide and dark brown, like his father's, looking at me.

I stroked his brow and sat by him. "I have sent to your mother George," I told him "she will want to know that you are unwell. You could go and stay with her, when you are better. 'Tis time for a visit anyway and Edward can go with you." He gripped my hands to show he heard but did not answer. Then the Doctor gave him a draught to help him sleep and we waited as the fever rose to a pitch.

The crisis came about midnight, why is illness always worse at night? I thought, anxious for the day and 'Johnny's' recovery but the fever did not break and leave him cool but weak, it burned him up and killed him.

We were all with him, me and Edward, Isobel and Hugh and of course the good Doctor Pencryth he seemed lucid, at the end just for a moment, and spoke, "Edward." Then he was no more.

We sat in shock round the bed and I found myself whispering, "No, no, it cannot be, he was so young, so strong, it cannot be." Then the Doctor and Isobel moved us away, to lay him straight and close his eyes. Edward was white with shock and grief and I held him close. 'Johnny' was his closest friend, more like an elder brother than a cousin and now he was gone.

As the sun rose I was back in the garden, pacing up and down across the grass, my shoes and skirt wet with the early morning dew. All I could think was "Why? Dear God in heaven, why?"

He would be washed and embalmed and dressed. Edward picked out 'Johnny's' best clothes, he would lie in the chapel for people to come and pay their respects and to wait for his mother.His mother, I started, with my lord away from home 'twas my duty to tell her that her son was dead. How, I shook my head to try and clear my thoughts, how was I going to tell her. What parent thinks to outlive their child? Especially a lad near full grown, almost a man, and so full of life as 'Johnny'?

As I paced back and forth I saw someone coming towards me, it was Hugh, whom Richard trusted and whom he had left, to help me run the castle he who had trained the boys in archery and weapons and knew them like his own sons. Who better to take the news to Lady Neville, I thought, than Hugh.

*   *   *   *   *

Anne

I was to go to London. George's mother had come to claim her son and to take him home, Edward had gone with her and Hugh and Isobel. I was summoned to London by my lord and also by the King. Edward had written a fair hand but his youth betrayed him, the wording of his letter stiff and formal in an effort to sound regal.

Would he learn his father's easy, relaxed way of ruling? Only time would tell. Meanwhile the factions had begun, even with his mother living in the Abbots Palace at Westminster Abbey, supposedly in sanctuary, still she succeeded in having her own courtiers round her son, daily. If Richard called a meeting at Baynards, Westminster Palace or Crosby Place, others would visit Edward at the Tower Palace.

I wondered as I packed my personal things, why Richard did not stop this. He has to learn to rule I know, I mused to myself but surely separate meetings meant factions and factions meant trouble for England.

I would travel in easy stages, visiting some of our homes en route; Sherriff Hutton would be my first stop. York of course and Pontefract, Bowles would be another and a visit to Walsingham's shrine to pray for the repose of 'Johnny's' soul and light a candle. I would also visit Fotheringhey and the monument to Richard's father and brother Edmund.

Thus I would fulfill our duties as lord and lady of our manors and also obey the King's and my husband's summons.

The journey took about ten days and I arrived at Crosby Place on 5 June to find Richard, who had moved from his mother's house that day, waiting for me.

Chapter 3
From Protector to King

Crosby Place

We sat in our room at Crosby place; a fire was laid but not yet lit. It was early June and quite mild, the evening was pleasant and blossom still hung heavy on the trees and scented the air.

Richard had sent for me to join him as soon as Edward V had been safely conducted to London. Edward was, even now, ensconced in the royal apartments of the Tower Palace, awaiting his coronation.

Edward V, I sighed heavily, who would have believed this when Edward, our King, Richard's brother had seemed so hale, so full of life? I shook my head as my thoughts spun round. How? Why? What? When? Although we had now been given the answers, all was not well. Suddenly Richard had lost his elder brother, I my brother-in-law and our Edward his Uncle. England? England had lost her King.

His son had lost a father albeit one he barely knew. Anthony, Earl Rivers had been closest to Edward, and Richard had confined him until the Council could decide how to act. The Earl was at our own Sherriff Hutton where he could enjoy our books and the beautiful gardens. Clearly the actions of all three men had been treasonable, what choice was there? I wondered, except to find them guilty to which there was but one punishment, death.

What had possessed Edward to allow such overwhelming Wydville influence over his son? So that we, his York side of the family, were looked on as strangers, by that son, ay, even as enemies of his family. For our new King's family had been 'til now his mother's. Who was behaving like a tigress at bay, defending her cubs. Why? I wondered and why had she deprived her son of the royal treasury?

Her family, true, were no longer in the prime positions for running the country. But none had been killed and no attempts had been made on their lives. Her son was King and though she would not be able to rule through him, no Queen of England had ever been allowed to do that, she would surely be honoured by her son, as his mother. What was Elizabeth so afraid of that she stayed in the Abbott's lodging claiming the right of Sanctuary? Knowing full well that it was the Sanctuary lodging itself that was covered by this right, not the Abbot's lodgings.

She had cowered there, in the Sanctuary house, when my father had rebelled against Edward the first time; she had been great with child then, with Edward V who was now on the throne. Then she had indeed known the rigours of Sanctuary with no bedding or clothes or even food for her children and the Londoners, who loved Edward well, had rallied to her side and provided for her and Edward's children until the King returned.

Edward had not forgotten and he had rewarded those merchants and butcher's well, who had so looked after the Queen and his babies. But this was not war; this was her son claiming his inheritance and Richard establishing himself as Protector until our new King Edward V was crowned.

I shook my head again, as I bent low over my tambour and examined the embroidery. I put it down and sighed and walked to the window to watch the last rays of the sun. Richard sat on the settle, legs outstretched, fondling his dog's ears and watching me beneath half shut eyelids.

The servants were due to light the fire and candles and to bring an informal supper and mead to warm us as the night air became chilled. A low hesitant knock came at the door and I turned, as it opened - no servant stood but Francis Lovell who I greeted gladly, as he came in our servant followed, lighting fire and candles whilst another brought supper and mead – and cups for us all. None of us spoke – Francis looked grave and my greeting had brought no warm answering smile but only a wry acknowledgement.

"Now what!" I Thought. Troubles had seemed to come thick and fast with Edward's death and now it seemed as if more news was being brought to shatter our peace. Richard looked at Francis – imperceptibly raising any eyebrow, he waited for Francis to speak. "I have had a visitor." Francis said, "with news that concerns you both deeply. He is with me, though sore afraid for his news is not good." Francis paused, "he fears to carry the blame for bringing it but does so for fear of God and his conscience." I had moved and sat by Richard holding his hand tightly. Richard did not speak but looked at Francis, waiting for him to continue. "Do we know this person, Francis?" I asked.

"Ay My Lady – 'tis Lord Stillington," he paused.

"The Bishop of Bath and Wells!" Richard interjected, incredulously, "and what would the Lord Bishop have to say that is of vital news to me?"

Bishop Stillington had been in the Tower with George, Richard's brother and was released by Edward a few months after George's death. Not a history to endear him to my lord.

"May he come in and tell you himself Richard?" Francis asked.

Richard nodded and Francis called a servant to bring the Lord Bishop to us. He was an elderly man – comfortably dressed (though not over rich, for a Bishop) and he came in hesitantly and sat on the chair that Francis held for him. Richard spoke into the silence. "Well? I believe you have news of some import – as it cannot wait 'til the morn…."He gestured for the Bishop to speak. Francis poured us all a cup of mead, "your news?" Richard prompted.

"My Lord," the Bishop licked his lips nervously. "My Lord, what I have to say is difficult. I have spent many days, nay weeks, agonising over it since the King's death. My knees are red and swollen with kneeling in prayer, asking for guidance, whether to keep silent, or whether to speak. I feel that my prayers have been answered, that I have been guided by God and mine own conscience. Hence I took the matter first to Master Lovell, knowing him to be your good friend and relying on his view of the matter – as to whether I should let it remain buried or to bring it before you, in all honesty." The Bishop paused, "and so My Lord you see me here, before you."

"So Francis," Richard interjected, half amused, "this is your doing, interrupting my few hours of peace. Is the matter really so important?"

"Ay Richard," Francis answered in a low tone, "I do believe it to be so – and the decision – what to do - can be none but yours."

"In that case," Richard spoke dryly, and gestured, "My Lord Bishop pray continue."

"Before I became Chancellor to the King, your brother, I accompanied him on many a battle and also in more leisurely pursuits, on his progresses round the country and on hunting trips. We visited many a Lord who was glad to put him up – many no doubt hoping a daughter or niece would catch his eye and would become his wife and Queen."

"Not Edward," Richard interrupted, "he would not be trapped so easily."

"Ay," the Bishop replied "unless such a one demanded marriage before she was bedded."

"And we all know the end of that story," Richard commented, "my sister-in-law, the dowager Queen of England, who hides behind the Abbots skirts with the treasury and half the Crown Jewels. Where is this leading to My Lord."? His tone was terse and impatient. Stillington looked at his Bishop's ring as if searching for an answer – then he spoke.

"The trouble is, my Lord, that the King," he took a deep breath, "the King had played that game before."

"What mean you?" Richard sat up straight – alert – his hand gripping mine until it hurt. Understanding was hovering in the room but was not yet manifest.

"The Lady Eleanor Butler, My Lord – Talbot's daughter, the Earl of Shrewsbury. She too was a young widow and truly virtuous – she would not bed with the King without being married to him," he paused.

"And?" Richard asked.

Stillington shrugged, "and so, he married her."

I watched the conflicting emotions on Richard's face, incredulity, disbelief, memories of Edward's conquests, confusion and finally resignation.

"If this be true," Richard spoke firmly, "you have proofs?"

The Bishop looked at him directly for the first time. "Ay, My Lord – for I presided over the ceremony myself."

*   *   *   *   *

Chapter 4
King Richard by the Grace of God!

They had left us to think, to put this startling news into some sort of perspective and to see what it could mean for the boy King and for us.

For me it was like a piece of a puzzle fitting into place or solving a riddle. It was the only explanation for Elizabeth Wydville's fear and may be, I thought but durst not say, for George's acting like the Heir to the throne, with Edward's two sons preceding him.

I thought of George's behaviour in the year prior to his execution. Of his own brother, the King, bringing the charges against him. Petty charges when George had committed treasons so many times. We had wondered why, this time, Edward could not allow his brother to live. Was this the reason? Had George chanced upon Edward's guilty secret? And she had died, poor Eleanor, in a nunnery, her and her stillborn child, convenient after Edward's second marriage. King's of England are not allowed to marry again whilst their first wife still lived and divorce is not allowed by our Holy Mother Church. Betrothal is as binding as marriage, so Edward, betrothed to Eleanor was married to her, as I had been to Edward of Lancaster, I sighed. Once done, it could not be undone, by commoner or King.

I wondered why he had not had a state marriage with Elizabeth, who had been taken on progress through the realm, as soon as she had been crowned. Once Eleanor was dead, it would have made all legal, and none would have queried it. He had insisted on her Coronation, a lavish affair it was, and though it did not appease the Council or my father, the commons had enjoyed the free wine and food. Eleanor had obliged him by dying, soon after his marriage was made public, and the Queen's Coronation. A wedding celebration would have gone down well. Why Edward, did you not act, did you honestly think no one would find out, or where you so sure of life that you thought to have Edward safely grown, and mayhap even crowned, before you left this life? Of course, that was why he chose Richard as Lord Protector, his ever-loyal brother, who accepted all Edward did, he would expect Richard to ensure his son ruled no matter what. Did he know Richard so little? Did he not remember Richard's 'damned conscience?' as had he called it himself. Did he honestly think that Richard would go against God's law and man's for Edward? The law you had shaped, Edward, and made good. Of all the foolish, selfish things you had done Edward, this was the worst. 'Selfish! Selfish! Selfish!' I cried out as my right fist punched my other hand. How dare he put us, put Richard, into this untenable position? What would Richard do?

Richard, of course did the only thing he could do, he called a meeting of friends and members of the Council to hear Bishop Stillington's testimony and see the proofs. Then he left it with them and we supped with his mother at Baynard's.

He told her, of course, she who loved Edward but knew his ways well, as she also knew Richard. He needed her guiding hand in this. If they offered him the crown instead of his nephew, to whom he had given his pledge, whom his brother Edward had placed directly under his care, what should he do?

In law he, Richard Duke of Gloucester was Heir to the throne. A position he had not looked for and did not want. The law was clear however, if the Council where convinced that Edward's boy's were bastard, they had to offer Richard the Crown. If not, Edward V would be crowned as planned, all the preparations having gone on apace and his robes of State almost ready. This is what Richard wanted; he looked at his mother earnestly; to bring the boy to the Coronation, to be his right hand if he wanted, and to hold the North for Edward V as he had for Edward IV. The revelation from Bishop Stillington was like a bolt of lightning into our world, what should come first? Love for his brother or his duty to the country? If the Council found Stillington to be presenting the truth, should he try and over ride the law of the land and the law of God to keep faith with Edward? If he were over ridden would they put George's son on the throne, a lad, poor boy, who was known to be half witted? Would it be like the early reign of Henry VI again, opening the door to unscrupulous men to drain the Crown of it's land and wealth, undoing all that Edward IV had done.

"What would you do Richard? In that event?"

"I would fight," he sighed, "fight to restore order and justice to the realm. We do not want to go down that road again."

"Exactly." Cecily looked at him firmly. "Edward brought stability to England. I never like that Wydville bitch I know, but she was Queen, and his wife. We would have honoured his son as King. This puts a whole different light on the situation. I am only surprised that she did not persuade Edward to make all right." She reflected momentarily, the continued, "however, she didn't and he didn't, whatever their reasons I don't think the Wydville woman will tell us now. Be sure she will shout loud enough if it is not true." She smiled, "maybe 'twill bring her out of the Abbott's lodge and what if you do not accept the crown, if offered? Edward is proved truly bastard, what about your own family, your own Edward, and Anne. What will be your place? Will you have one? You could not remain Lord Protector even if it were George's lad they put on the throne. Would you have the council give the crown to someone else, someone less honest than you, less able than you? You have many qualities, Richard, use them for the good of your country, there will be plenty to help and advise. Plenty who know the court rules and political games for you to turn to. Surround yourself with honest men, men you know from your time in the north, men you can trust." She appealed to me. "What say you Anne? Should he not take the crown, if Stillington's revelation is proved true?"

My reasoning, however, had not brought me so far along the road she travelled and her words had made me recoil in horror within myself. For if Richard accepted the crown I would be queen, it was too much and I walked out into the garden, which was sideways on to the river. It was evening and the sun glinted on the water turning it into liquid gold and tinting the sailing craft in golden hues, I had a clear view from the terrace on which I stood and all was serene and beautiful.

As I walked down the steps I prayed for an answer and as I gazed round the garden I saw a white rose tree suddenly bathed in golden sunlight. Was this the answer? I do not know but I suddenly became sure of my response to Cecily and to Richard as well.

I walked back into the room where Richard sat, now sprawled in familiar attitude with his mother's dogs at his feet. She sitting quietly reading her missal, letting him think. I stood in front of him, my hands clasped in front of me like a little girl. "Richard," he looked up, "have you reached a decision, My Lord?"

He looked quisikly at my formal address. "No Anne," he sighed, "no my love, I have not." I drew a deep breath.

"Well I think you must do it." I paused, "we must do it." He did not answer, just looked intently at me. "Your mother is right, my love, Edward is already declared a bastard, he can no longer be King no matter what you decide. So who else, if you refuse, could take the crown, not George's son, so whom? Bockenham perhaps? No Richard it must be you. To keep England safe and on the path your brother set out for her, it is the only answer. The people know you or they know of you and your loyalty to Edward, the battles you have won the diplomacy succeeded in, even with the Scots," he smiled at that. "You will rule well, govern well, as you have in the north and like our northerners the people will learn to trust and love you. Oh Richard I do not want this either, to be queen. I want to return to Middleham, to see my son grow and learn his craft to govern the north, as his father has. God it seems has other plans for us, and Edward will still learn his craft of course but now he will learn to govern not one part of England but all of her." I stopped and knelt before him and we held one another.

Cecily came and stood by us, "Well Anne," she said, "you never cease to amaze me. Come here my dear." She raised me to my feet and kissed my cheeks. "She is right of course, Richard. You must do it. Never think that Edward would not understand. He always knew your 'damned conscience' as he put it, would get in the way. That's why you were better in the north than at court. You must rule, my son." She spoke gently and reaching up stroked his cheek "for you will rule well. Besides," more brusquely now, "you still have the care of Edward's sons and his other offspring. They will have need of your care, Richard," she warned.

Then she smiled, wished us well and left us to talk on our own. As her children had grown up she had become more of a recluse and I found myself admiring this strong but pious woman. Who could allow her children lead their own lives and advise them impartially when needed. I hoped that I could be as strong and as fair as she.

*　　　　　*　　　　　*　　　　　*　　　　　*

Chapter 5
Edward Prince of Wales

It had all happened so quickly. First my father was declared Lord Protector, then 'Johnnies' death and my trip with his body, home to his mother.

She had come for him on receiving the news, which Hugh had taken to her and it was Hugh and I who would accompany her and her son on his last journey.

Mother was sent for, by my father, from London, we had had no time to tell him of my cousin's death, his ward. Mother would send a messenger on ahead and give papa the details on her arrival in London.

Father was staying with his mamma, my great aunt, Cecily, at Baynards.

He had written my mother that he would ask John Paston to rent his house, again, at Crosby Place. Mother was pleased, she loved Crosby Place and it would give her and my father some privacy away from Westminster, whilst they were in London. "I will have to stay for Edward's coronation, of course." She said to me, "and help your father and the queen dowager to reach some agreement. Your cousin's family should be with him when he is crowned, celebrating. That Wydville woman," she positively stamped, "I will never understand her."

Now, two weeks later and an urgent message had arrived from my father's scribe, with a postscript in papa's own hand. Edward, my cousin, had been proved bastard by the Bishop of Bath and Wells. Bourchier had been to talk to the dowager queen for confirmation or denial, with copies of the documents to be laid before Parliament, documents the King's council had already seen. She had not answered them, only sat, with her daughter's grouped around her, father said. Inclining her head only once to show that she understood but saying neither ay or nay. With the proofs and the dowager queen's silence, the council had decided that mine uncle, the late King had, in fact, been betrothed to another before his marriage to mistress Grey and that therefore their marriage was illegal.

"My son," my father had writ in his own hand. "The enormity of this will not escape you, I know. By rights my brother George's son should have the crown but apart from his father's attainder, which we, as a council could reverse, Edward has been kept so ill by my lord of Dorset; that he is too unworldly and ill educated to hold England stable.   Therefore it has been put to me that I should accept the crown. The council needs to act and I needs must make a decision to accept or no. If I say ay, then you, my son, will be Edward, Prince of Wales.   I know you are readying yourself to come for your cousin's coronation, if we are crowned in his stead, we will progress to York and see you there.   I would not have you meet your cousins in London under such circumstances." Gloucestre, Crosby Place, London.

Now the unthinkable had indeed happened, the council had called a parliament and a paper was drawn up declaring my father's right to the throne. The pulpit, which stood outside St. Paul's Cathedral, had been used by Dr. Shaa, brother to the Lord Mayor, to inform the citizens of the awful fact.   Mine uncle's pre-contract, or betrothal, had been to Lord Shrewsbury's daughter, the Great Talbot, he was my hero and I had heard about all his battles in France. My poor cousins, I thought, to be King and a King's brother one minute, the next mere Dukes, lords of substantial manors, true but not like being the King.

I would now be Prince of Wales, my father would organize my investiture I knew, although I knew not when. It did not seem real; I was learning to manage my father's estates, at Middleham, but England! And my mother, how would she see all this, how would she feel?

She had already nearly been queen once, I knew. Betrothed to Edward of Lancaster, son to Henry VI but he had died in battle, quite bravely by all accounts and mama had not been attainted as had her father and uncle.

As with her sister, my aunt Isobel, Edward IV had been lenient and indulgent towards his two brothers. Isobel was already married to mine Uncle George and mother was allowed to marry my father.

Mama often told me the story, how papa had rescued her from the cook-shop and how he had rode away with her, 'like a true knight' she would always say.

Now the coronation date was set, papa and mamma would be King Richard III and Queen Anne. Mamma had written quickly, once the decision was made and the official recognition given by Parliament.

"My sone greetings, Edward I wit you be well. This day has Parliament sanctioned your father as King of England. I write this to you hardly believing it to be true. 'Twas not what we expected when we came to London, as well you know. My dear sone the coronation is to be held on July 6. Pray for us and we will hope to see you soon for your investiture as Prince of Wales at York. Father and I will make our first progress through the kingdom to include the north, so that we may see you. I will return with you to Middleham, via Sherriff Hutton, who knows when I will have chance to spend time in these places again. Keep you well and keep to your studies, an I know you will." Then, in her own hand, 'I am minded to sign, Anne, Queen of England, just to see how it feels, Mama, given at Westminster.'

Hugh also had a letter, from papa on how I must keep to my studies now that I was heir to the throne. I sighed heavily; being King suddenly seemed to me to be a heavy responsibility.

*   *   *   *   *

"A dozen white roses please." We were in Middleham and had asked the vicar of St. Akelda's if we might honour the Coronation Day of Richard III and Queen Anne, by placing a dozen white roses in a vase by the altar. There was to be a service during the day and a play about Richard in the evening.

A vase had been left out for us to use and I arranged the roses plus one I had picked from outside the church. I don't remember much about the service only that, as we prayed, I felt an overwhelming sadness overcome me.

*   *   *   *   *

They came the next day, the council, to hear Richard's decision. Announcements were made at Paul's Cross by Reverend Shaa to impart the news to the populace. Bockenham had spoken for Richard to take the crown, in Westminster Hall, though when Richard heard later that he had imputed Edward's legitimacy and thereby his mother, he was not best pleased. He put it down to Harre's exuberance, but I wondered, I did not trust any of them yet, they had not been tried and tested. God would bring that time, and then what? I wondered, how loyal would Harre and all of these new friends prove then? It was not that long ago that Richard had foiled the plot against his life. Not by Harre and William, he reminded me, no not by them, I agreed, not this time.

Meanwhile the Londoner's were stunned, as we had been at the news of Edward's pre-contract to Lady Eleanor. They could barely take in that the council had agreed to offer Richard, Duke of Gloucester, the crown, though all knew his worth, they did not know the man. Richard had been to court only when necessary, none of them really knew him, only that Edward, had trusted him completely and referred to him as "my right arm."

This the people did know and would trust Edward's judgement up to a point, whilst waiting for Richard to prove himself. There was a need to act quickly, the council told them, England could not be left without a monarch, all would be chaos. So they had deliberated over many days and nights and had determined to offer lord Richard the crown.

They had no great certainty of the outcome of this offer, although all of them had urged Richard to say 'Yes', none knew but his mother and myself what his answer would be. Bockenham had been most aggrieved at Richard's refusal to share his deliberations, even with him. He had supported Richard as Lord Protector and would support him as King, he declared vehemently.

Francis was too wise to expect Richard's confidence until Richard was ready to give it. So the Lords had urged the Londoner's to go with them and persuade Richard to accept the Crown, in hopes that if he was going to refuse, seeing such a crowd might persuade him to change his mind, they did not know Richard.

He had dressed carefully, knowing that he also had to look like a King, now the decision was made. None of this would involve me. No one expected Richard's wife to have a say in any of this. I was unknown at Court and to the London citizens; I was Richard's wife and expected to follow my husband.

"If only they knew." Richard held me gently. "I would not and could not have done this with out you. I will need you now Anne," he continued, "more than ever. If I forget to tell you how much, please remember these words and my love for you." We heard the noise of hundreds of people entering the courtyard and I walked to the top of the stairway with him, glad not to be placed in front of all these people, yet.

As he began to descend Cecily came to my side and slipped her arm around my waist. "We will watch together, an it please you?" She said and I squeezed the hand at my waist gratefully.

Bockenham was there, now a member of the Council as Richard had recognised him, whilst he was Protector, as the foremost Magnate of the Land next to himself. Once Richard was King, Harre Bockenham would replace my Father in importance, I thought, forgetting that the Wydville's had done that long since.

My Lord of Gloucester," a voice rang out clear and true, to be heard by all. Bockenham, I thought! "As you know most serious concerns have been brought to the Council by the Bishop of Bath and Wells. He has shown us proof, beyond doubt, of a marriage contract by King Edward IV to Lady Eleanor Butler – daughter of the great Lord Talbot, Earl of Shrewsbury. This contract was still in order when our late King Edward IV of that name married Mistress Elizabeth Grey, known as Wydville, Queen of the said Edward IV.

Although the said Eleanor subsequently did die, in a Nunnery, the aforesaid King Edward IV and Queen Elizabeth did not go through any subsequent marriage service or ceremony thus making their offspring bastards all."

He paused for effect and then continued. "It is for this reason – and after much deliberation – that we the Council of England and foremost Magnates of the realm ask you - My Lord – as heir to England's throne to accept the Crown and duties of Kingship. What say you, My Lord?"

Richard was half way down the staircase and the early morning sun came glinting over the parapet, dazzling his eyes – as he told me later. He took two steps further to avoid the sun and so it glinted on his dark hair. I heard a low gasp, "Look, look, the sunlight – it look's like a halo – Edward's sun, it must be a sign," the crowd murmured.

Then Richard spoke. "My Lord's and citizen's – I have deliberated on this question also. This was an honour I had never expected to be mine but for your sake and for England's I will accept my duty."

The relief on the face of the council and Lords was obvious. There was no shouting, or cheering, the reason Richard would now be King was still too raw, too awful but I saw people hugging one another. Richard's horse was brought for him to ride to Westminster for he needed to accept and be accepted sitting on the great stone throne with the stone of Scone under it and to be confirmed as King by the Archbishop. He could not go to the Royal Apartment's, in The Tower for Edward and his brother Richard Duke of York, were still there. So he would go on to Westminster Palace, where I would join him later.

Meanwhile someone would have to inform Edward that he was no longer King and also the dowager queen.

*   *   *   *   *

Richard elected to tell his nephew himself. He forbade Harre or Francis to go with him. I think he expected tears and tantrums but no, Edward may no longer be King but his Plantagenet blood showed in his bearing and his manner.

"He drew himself up," Richard told me, "looking so dignified," he smiled dryly, "every inch a King, and said, 'So uncle you have usurped our throne.' What could I say? For in truth that is what I have done, Anne, against my brother and against his son. Yet what else could I do after Stillington's confession? No wonder George had to die this time," he said suddenly and apropos of absolutely nothing. So, he had realised too, I thought, glad that it was not only I leaping to conclusions. "Then, young Richard spoke. 'We understand Uncle,' he said to me seriously, 'Our father did wrong and we must pay for it.'

I saw Edward's eyes fill with tears. He took the King's seal off his hand and gave it to me, then turned his back, as I stood looking awkward. "It will take time uncle, but Edward does not know you as I do, having been in Ludlow so long. We will be your loyal subjects." Then he too turned away to comfort his brother and I, King though I may now be, felt like a shuffling knave unworthy to be in their presence.

I had expected the Wydville screams and accusations, as their mother used to do to Edward – when the whole Palace would hear. But no, they are true Plantagenets, Edward would have been so proud, would to God he had made their throne secure. I will go to them again, before we are crowned, they are good boys and will make fine men. Maybe we can send them to Middleham to join Edward at his lessons? So they do not have to witness me in their father's place." His voice trailed off to a whisper. He sat, not sprawled as was his usual want, but tense with lines appearing on his face that had not been there before. He had only been King for a day.

*   *   *   *   *

Chapter 6
Abbott's Lodge - Westminster

"Is it true?" All her daughters had come to her but it was the eldest who spoke. Elizabeth, named for her stood straight and tall facing the woman who was their mother and had been queen and that woman sat, sideways on, not to be faced by their looks of unbelief and horror at the news. The announcement had been made at Paul's Cross by the Reverend Shaa – known as Dr. Shaa, for he had been to Rome and studied Divinity at the University there.

The woman, who had been Queen, sat straight and still, not moving; the events of the past months playing back to her. Her own boy had been declared bastard and the Council would ask Richard of Gloucester to take the Crown. Her impotence ate into her as her friends had brought the news of what would occur today. She must come out of 'sanctuary' they begged her, refute the imputation to her, to Edward her Lord and their marriage.

She sat then, much as she did now, silent, unmoving, unable to dispute that which she knew to be true. She replayed the many conversations with Edward, remembered begging him to re-dress the situation. To execute Stillington on some trumped up charge but he would not. It seemed that Edward too had a conscience, damn him and so the secret which had been kept like a viper, close to their bosoms, had reared its head and bit.

She had really underestimated Edward's brother; mealy mouthed Gloucester, the country bumpkin had outwitted her at every turn. Her bid to rule through her son had failed, dismally she had to admit to herself, and now Stillington had played his hand and Gloucester would take the throne. All was lost, because of that simpering Butler woman.

Eleanor had been wise enough to say nothing, when Edward announced to his council that he would need no foreign wife as he was already married. She had gone into a convent, her and her child but she had died and Edward had the child brought to Westminster Palace to be brought up with his own children.

The girl did not know who her mother was, no one did and that is how it would stay. Just one of Edward's by blows, the court had sniggered, and soon forgot. No one, it seemed, thought to question why this by-blow was more important than all the others, so important that Edward wanted her brought up in his own household.

Small and delicate at 7 years of age she looked younger, and so they had said that she was only 5 years old, so that no one would make the connection. Born in the convent she had known no other life until her mother died. Edward had paid for her keep and continued to pay the Nun's to care for her. No one knew, they thought the child had been a boy and still born. Then Edward had visited her and it had all changed, pretty and delicate he feared for her and his conscience smote him and so he took her up on his horse and brought her home to me. Her mouth twisted, and I had to wear it, bringing up her brat, had to keep the secret for my own children's sake.

Her children, all known to be bastards now. She turned suddenly towards her eldest, she had not answered her question, hand's twisting in her lap she spoke one word, "Yes."

It was more of a whisper and they could barely hear. Elizabeth of York spoke again, "What?" It was a question and exclamation and her mother repeated herself, more clearly now, so that they could all hear. "Yes, yes, it is true."

She offered no explanation, no apology. They did not expect her too – she was still mama and still Dowager Queen of England and they still held her in awe, and they loved her. One announcement from Paul's Cross may change many things in their lives but it would not change this, or erase their natural obedience to her as their mother.

They had seen her laugh and cry, be happy and be angry, seen their parents argue and make up, had seen their abiding love, despite their father's mistresses. She and Edward had shown them such love, for they were born of their great love, a love that, Edward had promised her, would conquer all. He would see his son grow to manhood and set him on the throne and retire to the background, as Henry II had done. He would not make the same mistakes of his ancestor, they would enjoy life; and Edward V would rule.

He had made one mistake, however, he had forgot he was mortal and that God might have other plans. He had died and left her – not as regent as they had agreed but had nominated his brother as Protector. 'Why, oh why Edward?' she groaned silently.

They had tried, her and her son, but her brother Anthony, unaware of the machinations and the politics had not been aware of the urgency of bringing the new boy King to London. He had tarried overlong at Ludlow had agreed to meet Gloucester at Northampton before her own messenger had met him on the road.

Anthony allowed himself to be directed by his sister, and his Queen, he owed her everything and their plans were laid. But someone had alerted Gloucester, he had been ready for them and their plans were overturned and lay in ruins about them. And now this! With her beautiful daughters standing about her, come to call her to account for their lost lives. No longer royal princesses just bastards of a King, they would have no standing now, no advantageous marriages, what had the future in store for them with Gloucester on the throne?

All were silent then a voice came from their midst, "and Edward and Richard? What becomes of them? Do they join us here? Or do we leave these quarters and go to them wherever the King decides to lodge them?" Elizabeth winced at the title so bestowed on the man who had taken her son's throne.

"Leave here? Leave here? How may we leave here, madam, how?" her anger spat and her children quailed.

Grace was used to her guardians temper and did not give ground, "but your son's, madam. We must safeguard their well being." Quiet she may be, Elizabeth thought but she would not be beat. Dark, like her mother, yet her bearing was from Edward and, like Edward, she would not be gainsayed. Grace waited, quietly for an answer, and all the young women, her lovely children, she knew waited for her answer.

For to them Gloucester was Uncle Richard, their father, they knew, trusted him completely. They had all been horrified at their mother's dash into the Abbott's lodging, calling it 'sanctuary'. They had wanted to stay at Westminster Palace to welcome Edward, did not understand the stripping bare of the royal apartments. It felt that their lives were being torn apart before their eyes. Even now they urged her to leave the 'sanctuary' as they had urged her to at least let Richard join his brother.

They did not understand, she thought, did not know what she had attempted against Gloucester (she would not call him King, never!), did not realise the danger they could all be in if Gloucester decided on retribution. He could take everything, titles, wealth everything and give them a pittance to live on. She had tried to rule the King and thereby England, why should Gloucester forgive? She knew that she would not.

Chapter 7
Queen Anne

They brought Edward to me straight away as Richard had ordered, relieved to at least be able to get Clarence's son away from Dorset's household. The Earl himself in hiding after his plot against Richard as Lord Protector, the Abbott's lodging would be no sanctuary for him, he knew and he would not kick his heals in the true sanctuary building which was nought but cold stone walls and floors.

Edward, at ten years, was tall and handsome like his father but there was a gentleness about him too that he had from my sister, Isobel. He was grave and quiet, well mannered but overly afraid to speak. He had been looked after, but not loved, or groomed to be at Court, and people over awed him. He was slow to learn, it was true but he was not stupid.

I wished that Antoinette had still been alive to ask her advice and to help me in those first few months, to cosset and comfort him. To give him what he had not had since his mother died, a feeling of being safe. Richard asked me what I thought and I told him straight. "Give him back his childhood, he is not needed at court, indeed would be terrified to take his place there. Let him go to Sherriff Hutton, establish a household for him to run, give him good advisors but most important my love, let him have some women in his household who will care for him and show him love. Let him learn at his own pace, not to be told he is stupid so that learning becomes a fearful thing. He needs to be encouraged to grow and not to be afraid of the world. He will run his own household most successfully I am sure, once he gains confidence."

Richard hugged me, "That I will." he replied, on our first progress. Once Edward is established as Prince of Wales, my brother's son will indeed have his own household. Sherriff Hutton is a good idea for Lincoln will be up there betimes and can help to school him. For he must have the skills to be Earl of Warwick and to manage his father's estates." His eyes twinkled, and he smiled broadly at my look and exclamation of astonishment. Then more seriously, stroked my cheek and asked, "you do not mind? Edward having your father's title and lands?" Mind, I thought, how could I mind, for Edward of Warwick was not his father Clarence, and he would do well. This I said and more to

Richard and hugged him my love over flowing at his care for this lad who had up until now been ignored by his family.

*   *   *   *   *

Coronation
5 July 1483

It was time, we were due to be crowned and tradition demanded that we walk from The Tower to Westminster Abbey. Bockenham and Norfolk had the ordering of the Coronation and this day we would ride through the streets of London to be housed in the Royal Apartments of the Tower Palace.

I was scared and a little excited too. Suddenly, I was Queen of England, how my father would have loved this. He would have seen only the power, not the danger, the riches not the cares. Mother knew, she would not come but would remain with Edward at Middleham and Cecily too begged to be excused. Her part was done, she felt, she had shown her support when we had stayed at Baynard's Castle. Now was our time, no one wanted to be gazing at the King's mother when there was a young Queen to admire, she had said. But I would miss the comfort of her presence.

Women I did not know, although I had heard of them, would hold my train, and pretend to be my friend, because I was Queen, only one, Lady Scrope, would indeed be that friend, tried and tested through the years.

Richard could not surround himself solely with our friends from the North, all the Magnates and their wives would have to be included. They would all be there, indeed it was such an affaire that Richard had asked for some of his Northern troops to help keep order. He had made it an offence to harass aliens, for these brought good trade, Richard also imposed a curfew of 10 p.m. to keep bawdy persons off the streets, so that people had less fear of being robbed. Of course some complained; they wanted the wine to flow all night as it had for Edward's coronation. There were twice the number in London at this time, however, all come to see us, and to wonder at the deposing of young Edward by his Uncle. We were an important event in the lives of all the populace and they wanted to see what they were getting.

As we came out of our royal apartments at Westminster Palace we could hear the noise of people waiting to see us. Richard had ordered me a lavish litter to ride in. Where I could see and be seen. He would ride ahead of me on his stallion and there would be henchmen to guard me. Five of the foremost ladies of the realm would ride on horseback, alongside my litter. I wondered just how much I would see, or if people would be able see me, but really they had come to see Richard III their new King.

Richard was dressed in deep blue with gold spun over it, wrought with nets and pineapples, and I similarly had been made a dress of the same hue, but with silver spun over the top so that it looked like spider's webs. We both wore long gowns of purple velvet furred with ermine and enriched with over 3,000 powderings of bogy shanks.

The roar of the Crowd was tremendous, and Bockenham's face was wreathed in smiles, he had done well, I conceded to myself. Though his horse pranced ahead of Richard's as if he were the King. Norfolk too was at the head of the procession and they would join us the next day, walking behind us, this time, as we made our way to Westminster Abbey to be crowned.

It passed in a haze, people were cheering and waving pieces of brightly coloured cloth and several of the merchants houses had Richard's flag draped in front of them to add to the colour and display. Our coat of arms, quartered with the Neville Cross where also displayed and I felt thankful in my heart. Tomorrow, of course we would only see displayed the arms of England.

The Tower

At last we were alone. Tradition demanded that the King and Queen, if there was one, were left alone the night before their Coronation and for this we were both thankful. Events had moved so quickly, too quickly for me, I had become used to Middleham and our own estates, which I had travelled round and organised in Richard's absences. This was all so sudden, so much larger and slightly overwhelming.

Cecily had advised me, "Take each palace as if it is your own Middleham," she said. "All castles and palaces are run in the same way. Do not be over awed; just remember though, that it is the same, only larger." She had smiled, "A sure way to offend is not to have enough food to feed them all." Then she went on, "remember they all have a Steward or Chamberlain who knows how it is done, ask for advice, they will love you for it."

Richard was stood looking out of the window. Was he remembering, I wondered, when he had visited his nephew here and he had been Protector to Edward V? He turned and smiled, "come my love let us get out of these fancy clothes and eat." We had often acted as each other's maid and manservant, and we did so now, not wanting to be disturbed.

We had kept with us those whom we always had when we stayed at Crosby Place. People who always travelled with us and who were familiar from Middleham.

We both decided that we had enough new faces, for the present, although we were sure that the Magnates and Lords would soon press for their sons and daughters to be our lords and ladies in waiting. Not tonight though, our last night together as Gloucester, we needed familiarity and quiet and friends.

*   *   *   *   *

To be crowned a Queen
6 July 1483

We awoke early, with Richard going into the dressing room to wash and robe ready for our walk to Westminster Abbey to be crowned. My maids came into our chamber to help me wash and dress and to brush my hair. We were to be dressed simply in white damask, our robes of state would be at the Abbey where we would be dressed after the Chrism was used to anoint us with oil and Richard would swear to be a just King and uphold the laws of the land. We had long purple coats, with trains, that we would put on at the Abbey door.

The walk from the Tower to Westminster Hall would be without ceremony. We would be dressed as any penitent or pilgrim might dress, coming to our God in due humility, to ask to live our lives in His grace, to do His will and be guided by His laws only, Richard, as King, would take the Oath that every Monarch took. From now to be bound by duty and love too look after his subjects and to honour the laws of the land.

I had sent for a copy of the Book of Hours, used by our royal cousin in Italy, and had caused to be added a special prayer for Richard. This I would present to him once we were King and Queen and ensconced in the royal apartments at Westminster Palace and on our own. I had chosen pieces from two psalms and had them written out as one prayer for him. He would face enemies I knew, as King, just as other King's, in the past, and in the present, he would need to ask God for His help and guidance and to be his shield.

Being King would not be easy as Henry IV had found. For Richard, who had a conscience to guide him I felt it would be doubly hard. He would want to do the best for all, poor and wealthy alike but how would the wealthy feel about it, I wondered. Hastings had seen his power being eroded and had changed from life long friend of York to traitor, for by trying to over turn Richard he was attacking Edward V who was in Richard's charge. To put the Wydville's back in power, to rule through the young King would not have served England.

Yet Richard's conscience had not let him take Hastings land or castles and his widow and her young lad would hold on to all that her husband had owned. Hasting's brother was still in Richard's entourage and no slight allowed or disparaging remark made, to him or his family.

I mused on this as my ladies helped me ready myself. I felt detached, as if I were watching myself get ready. Talking and laughing with my ladies, only one was family and a friend to trust, come with me from Middleham, her I vowed I would keep with me always. Was this really me? Putting on the beautiful but simple white damask skirt and top? It did not seem real, that I, Anne Neville would at the end of the day be Queen of England.

Suddenly Richard was by my side, his arm held out his eyes twinkling, as if he knew my thoughts. "My Lady?" was all he said, however and we made our way out of the Tower Palace to walk to Westminster Hall, as tradition demanded.

This his brother Edward had done at his official coronation and later Elizabeth Grey, once he had informed the council of their marriage. She had been Queen for over 20 years and despite her good works had been harsh and not much loved by the people.

A broad ribbon of red cloth was ready laid for the procession which made its way to Westminster Hall and then, barefoot we walked the last, to the doors of Westminster Abbey.

I would not be as she had been, I vowed as we began to walk, I would not claim the queen's gold, as she, and other queen's had done, there would be enough money from my own estates, I would take from no one.

*   *   *   *   *

Chapter 8
Richard

The Progress

The decision to move the Princes to Sherriff Hutton was mine. I realised very quickly that the only way to ensure their safety was to spirit them away. It was vital to move the boys, not only for their own safety but to remove any focal point, they may be perceived as being, for unscrupulous people to use them and to try and re-establish Edward on the throne. For my rule to remain stable and for Edward's laws to be continued and to establish mine own, the Princes had to be put into a place where they would be hidden and safe.

There was, of course, the dim threat of Tudor over in Brittany, he had styled himself Duke of Richmond; the title Edward had given to me; because his father, Edmund Tudor had had that title on his death. As only princes of the blood royal can bear the title Duke, the inference was clear, but the man was of bastard Beaufort stock, so, like my nephew, could not be King.

Too many people had access to the Tower and though the boys were no longer in the Royal apartments, this in itself posed a dilemma, for any one could get in to them.

The Tower was constantly besieged by the Londoner's selling their wares and they had become used to the boys coming out to choose some sweetmeats or comfits from their trays, or even a hot meat pie, boys are always hungry.

I confided in Buckingham and of course Brakenbury, for I could not take the boys on progress until we began to head up North. I would have to send someone to get them from The Tower, in disguise and to bring them to me, at Warwick. Edward of Warwick, would be with me he would come to Pontefract and see Edward inaugurated as Prince of Wales at York Cathedral.

Two more boys would not be remarked on, I hoped. They would have to have their distinctive blond hair, cut and would be dressed as squires of the body so that they could mingle with their cousins un-remarked.

Buckingham's part was to ensure that no one knew any different. I put him in charge of the Tower, not to keep the boys safe, as was commonly thought, but to confuse and baffle any who may wish them or myself harm, by using them. He was to stay at the Tower until I returned to London - the transporting of the boys to safety was my responsibility and mine alone.

The Earl of Lincoln was at Sherriff Hutton, running the Council of the North, between there and Sandal, my father's Castle. He would bring my son, Edward to Pontefract to meet us and we would all travel to York together for his investiture. Two more in my sons company, I hoped would go un-remarked or noticed, my household I knew would ensure their anonymity and safety.

We were at Gloucester when Buckingham caught up with me. I was angry – his place was in London as arranged - his way of protecting the boys was to keep the façade going at The Tower, for as long as was feasibly possible. To fend off any questions and help keep the situation stable until the Tudor and his French allies could be dealt with, or anyone else who may wish them harm

We had a blazing row – 'who gave him permission to leave his post?' I demanded, 'not I' he just did not get it - he had betrayed my trust and my friendship. The boys were to join our progress at Warwick now my carefully laid plans were in danger, all due to Buckingham.

I had written to Brackenbury already to inform him that the queen would meet the boys at a designated spot as she rode from Windsor to Warwick. They would, ride with my messenger, and my good friend John Tyrrell, who had accompanied the queen's mother from Beaulieu to Middleham. He would do the same again and my nephews would be just two of his retinue. They would then join the queen, as escort, from Windsor and would meet her on the way. The Spanish ambassador was also due and would also ride with Anne to Warwick Castle the more the merrier, I thought, two boys could hide well with such a retinue.

First, I had to gain permission from Elizabeth Wydville, for she would raise a hue and cry if any rumours of her son's disappearance filtered in to her, via friends and supporters. She must know her sons were safe, and that she would have secret contact with them.

If she would come out of sanctuary, at a time agreed on by us both, she could name her own terms, to save face. It was all in the timing to ensure no one looked to deeply or wondered why the dowager queen had suddenly put herself and her daughters into my hands. It had to look as if she had won and I was being forced to accede to her demands. All would be revealed once England's peace was assured and the Tudor defeated. Her children were also Edward's, my brother, and I would pledge not to disadvantage them, but to treat them as royal princesses. The youngest could live at Sherriff Hutton too and the eldest could come to court or live with her at Grafton Regis, her marital home with her first husband Lord Grey. Her daughters too would have dowries as befitted their station and could marry for choice, I would force no marriage for expedience on them. How could I deny them the same chance of happiness that I knew with Anne?

All this I had set in motion, all this George had put at risk by his selfishness. Suddenly I saw him; a man I had trusted above all; for the selfish, greedy person he really was. He would put all at risk for his own end, to do as he wanted, rather than as his King commanded. Suddenly I saw Edward's reasons for not promoting George to his council, as his rank demanded. I had been overwhelmed and blinded by events. Something Edward would never have allowed of himself. I had much to learn I wryly admitted to myself, biting my lip and playing with my rings as I tried to decide what to do now?

The row culminated in me reminding this arrogant lord what he owed his King. I told him to cool his heels at his castle in Wales. I would send for him, in time but I added in my time.

1484

Whilst Grafton was made ready, Elizabeth decided to stay at the Abbott's Lodge. I had warned Richard that she would not come to court with her daughters. It would be cruel to expect her to watch us in Edward's place and her son's. Despite Richard's fairness to her, Elizabeth had still been in touch with the rebels led by Bockenham, the Wydvilles ay and the Beauforts. Yet he allowed her and her family to remain free, assuring her of her son's good health and well being at Sherriff Hutton. Once her eldest daughters had come to court, in March, we presented them as princesses of the blood royal, so to be treated by all. We decided that when we went north again, they could accompany us and visit their other sisters and brothers, as well as their many cousins, at Sherriff Hutton.

Chapter 9
Elizabeth of York

She was tall and fair to look on, much like her father I mused and hoped nothing like her mother. Elizabeth Wydville had, at last, left the abbots lodge in Westminster Abbey and placed her hands in fealty in Richard's. She had accepted her children as bastards and Richard as King, why? Because Richard had sworn, by the old Norman laws, promising her everything she wanted and I wondered if this was wise. The Wydville woman at court - I shuddered - but no Elizabeth had asked for and been granted, Grafton and a generous pension, with her daughters placed as royal wards and the eldest Elizabeth with her sister, Cecily, being allowed a place at court. Royal as Edward's daughters and Richard's nieces with even Edward's bastard daughter Grace being offered a place, and she wanted, to our surprise she declined and elected to accompany Elizabeth to Grafton.

It always surprised us that Elizabeth had accepted Edward's daughter, true I had accepted Richard's children as my mother had accepted Margaret, but generosity was not a well-known feature of Elizabeth's nature.

So we made a family in the royal apartments of Westminster. It must have been strange for the girls, seeing Richard and I in their parent's place. I came upon her once, the eldest, Elizabeth sitting in our apartments, formerly Edward's, the tears running unchecked down her cheeks. I sat and held her until her sobs subsided, how hard, I thought, to go from being in the line of succession to being declared bastard, not only by her most favourite uncle, but also by her mamma. I wondered why Edward had not thought to enact a second marriage ceremony once Eleanor Butler had, so conveniently died. So much heartache, so much upset to all our lives, would never have happened.

From this time on Bess and I became firm friends. She had been wary at first, not like her sister Cecily but then she was the eldest and most like both of them, inheriting Elizabeth's beauty and golden hair and Edward's grace. Gradually, as the months passed and Richard's decree was acted upon by all and due respect was given to Edward's daughters some of the shock and pain was alleviated. The hurt in their eyes lessened, as did the bewilderment. They spent time both at court and at Sherriff Hutton. Which I called to myself 'the children's castle' as we had given it over to our nieces and nephews, it was a safe haven as well as somewhere to grow, away from court. We had always felt that court life was not for children.

Edward of Warwick was managing the estate well with his cousin Lincoln's guidance and of course, unbeknown to any, his cousin Edward, the lord bastard, as he became known, lending a hand.

*   *   *   *   *

They let me enter the royal apartments with no query. Of course they did, uncle Richard had ordered that I was to be treated as a royal princess, as I had been when papa was alive. I wanted to see, to make sense of it all, after nearly two years restricted to the abbot's lodgings, where mother had dragged us unceremoniously before Edward and Uncle Richard had reached London.

I had been seventeen years of age and I did not understand, no more did any of us. Edward was King, uncle Richard Protector, what was there to run from? We took everything from our apartments, furnishings, beddings and drapes as well as clothes and jewellery, and mother had dumped us all in the abbot's palace. This was not sanctuary as it had been in Warwick's day when he was after our blood and papa's throne. Then we had run with nothing; to live in the sanctuary tower, a horrible place; awaiting news of papa's return. Mamma had been heavily pregnant with my brother Edward and there, in sanctuary he had been born, heir to England's throne. Mamma had been dignified throughout our ordeal, and the London merchants and butchers had seen us clothed and fed, had brought us beds and bedding, firewood and rushes for the floor. We knew papa would come for us and so did they, and they knew he would not forget them, nor did he, rewarding all who had helped us so. Now he was dead, gone, never to return in pomp with an army at his back and Edward my little brother was King. "Why mamma?" I asked her time and time again, "Why are we running away from Edward?"

Now Uncle Richard is King and mamma has reached an agreement with him. She had signed a piece of paper, virtually an admittance of father's pre-contract, and my uncle had signed too, promising us all honourable marriages of our own choosing and dowries befitting those of royal blood. "And Edward?" I asked, "and Richard?"

"They still have their titles," mamma had snapped "let them finish their education and be grateful for their lives and their desmesnes. Let them be grateful, that 'tis Richard on the throne," she added darkly, "He has a great sense of family, has Richard. He begged for Clarence's life, despite all the harm done by George to him and Anne. He is a fool," she spat, "but at least I know my children to be safe under his rule." She would not stay at court, however but took the pension my Uncle gave her and her much loved Grafton Manor. I did not know then that I would only see her once more, and then only for a few brief months.

The royal apartments were different of course, and yet the same. The same white rose and sunne in splendour hangings added to these was my uncle's own livery sign of the white boar, the red Neville saltire on a white background and velvet murrey and blue bed hangings. Like papa my uncle showed his York inheritance, coupled with my Aunt's Neville livery and maintenance.

Papa of course, had been eager to show mamma's de la Pole links to the house of Luxembourg via my grandmother. The bed now had similar soft furs, as papa had once had for warmth and smooth silk sheets. Thick rugs adorned the floor and a large table was strewn with papers quills and inkwells. The main difference was that my aunt and uncle shared this room. Mamma and papa had had separate rooms, only shared at papa's behest. Even I could not walk into papa's rooms at certain times, in case a mistress was present. Nevertheless, I spent many happy hours with papa and his dogs, often watching him work whilst I stitched a tapestry or embroidered some new collar or cuffs.

It was strange seeing a woman's mirrors and face creams, with undergarments and dresses in the dressing room, cloaks and shoes, perfumes and combs. A book was open on the window seat, a silk kerchief next to it, all signs of my aunt's presence.

I sat by the desk, unaware of the tears coursing down my cheeks, and that is how she found me.

Chapter 10
The Princes

I remember him setting off in the early morning light with Frances and a few body squires. He was King of England but rode incognito, in leather and hose, disguised, not for his safety but theirs.

No longer did the Tower Palace ring with their happy laughter or the gardens with the noise of their quoits or bowls, or arrows at the butts. No longer could the people of London tempt them with their wares or watch them ride through the streets on their ponies all trapped with velvet. He had spirited them away, my Richard, to keep them safe and now word had come that Edward, his brother's son, was dying.

This lovely boy with gilt hair, like his mother, shoulder length as a man's was worn, had but made his 12th birthday, when as the leaves fall so his life was falling from him. It was expected, constantly attended by my own physician, his jaw, which had constantly given him pain and trouble, now erupted with foul smelling poisons pouring from his suppurating flesh.

*   *   *   *   *

Our first progress
We had left London in late summer and I, desperate to spend time with my own son at Middleham, had begged my lord's leave to return there. I remember my logic, 'the people did not want to see me, it was he, their King they wanted to meet, to get to know and understand, a wife, albeit his queen would be a distraction. The time was too short, too important, and the people needed to see him, and only him, leaving me free to visit my son, his heir, at our most favourite of homes, Middleham'.

The reason he agreed was not through my carefully couched arguments but because my travelling on to visit Middleham would take me to Sherriff Hutton, where I could check on our wards and add two more, without comment or the knowledge of the world or our enemies. So we had parted he towards Nottingham and I, with my ladies and household to Sherriff Hutton with the boys dressed as squires and their distinctive hair coloured by acorn juice and cut to the appropriate length and style. The boys agreed to all, thinking it great fun, not realising that this would save their lives, they played their parts and did exceeding well.

As part of my retinue they galloped with me up through the gates of Sherriff Hutton our lovely manorial castle with its beautifully laid out gardens for the 'children' as I termed them all, to play in and enjoy. Places for the girls to sit and embroider outside when the weather was pleasant or to play their musike. As children they had to learn but life is precious and I wanted them all to enjoy theirs.

Now Edward, who had seemed so well, though I knew him to be in pain at times, was dying. I had known that the opium had been increased but Edward had concealed his true pain and now the physicians could not save him. A disease was rotting his gums and lower jaw and there was nought any could do. My lord, who had also come to Middleham to see his son, now rode as if his horse had wings for word had come from our nephew John that he feared his cousin was dying.

We could not go as a household, or indeed as ourselves. This would point our enemies towards Sherriff Hutton and our duty, Richard's duty, was to protect his brother's children and his sons were most at risk. Henry Tewder had declared his intention of wresting the crown of England from its King and of marrying Elizabeth, Edward's eldest. Richard took the news from his spies seriously and if true it was a death warrant for Edward and Richard, for how could Tewder hope to take the crown and marry Elizabeth with Edward's sons still alive?

Now Edward was dying, far from his mother, though at least his sister's were all with him. Richard too, having galloped fast and furious, arrived in time to comfort and hold him until the end.

* * * * *

"Judith! How nice to see you." My feelings were genuine. Not really in contact anymore, Judith and I had worked together and supported one another at work in some personal and bad times, so it was a real pleasure to see her. I wondered how she had been; she looked very well.

"Oh, I'm fine now." She answered.

"Now?" I queried. "Have you been ill?"

"Oh yes," she answered and explained that her new dentist has insisted on a full x-ray of her mouth, when he had taken over the practice. I knew what she meant as he was also my dentist and had a new super-duper x-ray machine.

"I had some pain, in my lower jaw," she told me, "and went to have my teeth checked, he saved my life."

I asked her how and it seemed that her teeth had been fine but that when they had x-rayed her jaw he had discovered a cancer in her gums. She had been in hospital for months and fortunately it had been cured. I did not ask any questions, assuming that the doctor's had cut away the cancer and used chemotherapy to kill it and prevent further cancer in her jawbone.

I had not realised that one could get cancer in the jawbone and said so. We agreed that the high profile cancers are in the breast or womb or bowel or even testicular but the jaw, I realised that I had never even considered that cancer could or would form there. "I'm okay now," she said, "but I owe that man my life, without him I would have died."

Chapter 11
Castle of Care

York Minster

It was not as I remembered from all those years ago, when Will had brought me, 'my memory must be playing tricks,' I thought. My memory of what I had thought was York Minster was of a Cathedral set up on a hill, there had been a fire, I remembered, and damage to the ancient ceiling. An escalator had reached down to a basement shop.

This was definitely not the same place, for here we were, in York at last, Richard's favourite city, and the Minster ahead of us, in the centre of city life.

This was were Anne had celebrated Corpus Christi, when she and her family had returned from Calais after spending her first 3 years of life abroad. We asked where the Richard III memorial window was and bought the plastic poster showing the white boars holding a shield of lions and lilies, the royal arms of England. We remembered that Richard and Anne had come to York on their final journey to Middleham to see their dead son. How had they felt, I wondered, how had they dealt with their grief, which, so reports said, had driven them almost mad.

*   *   *   *   *

He was gone now and all was spoilt! There was nowhere to go, nowhere to hide, there was only despair, despair, despair! 'Edward….!' As the keening cry rang out I jerked as he touched my arm. "Are you alright?" he was concerned, I seemed miles away, he told me, lost. I nodded and he led me out of the Minster door, into the warm sunshine.

*   *   *   *   *

Nottingham

The castle was still intact, building work was going on - re-building areas, which had long ago fallen - but the main part of the castle was still there. We walked round it - the now low wall came straight down on to the cobbled pavements which had been left in tact next to the castle, all was part of the town's history.

A green park surrounded the castle and we had to walk across it to gain entrance. We paid for our tickets at the gate house and asking for a guide book I also asked what information they had on Richard III and his Queen Anne Neville, who had stayed there. They looked at us blankly, no knowledge of the castle's history, they just 'worked there'. "Typical." I was fuming, I could not see how anyone could work in an historic building and not know its history. I watched him as we walked, waiting for him to 'pick up' on anything, as he had at Bosworth, to see if he could get any feelings of the momentous events of 500 years ago. Nothing.

"How do you feel?" I asked, "Fine." Came the reply, "don't you feel anything?" "No, I feel fine." His head was in the air as he looked about and we came to a bank of steps and began to climb. The steps led up to the top to what had presumably been the courtyard but which now had benches for visitors, who dared the steep climb, to rest on, once the top was achieved.

"Ooooow!" the pain hit me midriff and felled me to the floor. "No, oh no," I gasped as if someone had punched me. I was doubled over on the steps, trying to hold on to the rail and to find somewhere to put my hand, to stop the pain. My breathing was shallow and came in gasps. I tried to regain control and take deeper breaths - it was no good - the physical pain swept over me, along with a feeling of anguish and deep, deep despair.

"Are you alright?" he asked and I nodded, this was not my pain I knew but despair and anguish from times past. He took my hand and we walked on up to the courtyard and the feeling left me, I was fine.

"Didn't you feel that?" I asked, after all he was the sensitive, not me, he had had all the feelings and emotions at Bosworth, he must have felt something - but he had not. Someone's pain and anguish had needed a woman, because it was a woman's pain and the sensitive this time had indeed been me.

Later, as we sat having something to eat, we looked at the guide to the castle. The place where I had collapsed was beyond the curtain wall, on a part of the mound that led to the moat, the wall and castle rising above. If this were so why would I have picked anything up at that particular point? Was I in actuality picking anything up, was this how Anne Neville had felt on hearing about the death of her son? I did not know.

Once home I dug out an old favourite on Richard III by P.W. Hammond and Anne Sutton. There was a picture of Nottingham Castle in about 1500, built across two hills, and the main gate, where we had bought our tickets could be seen and a wall to where the main tower or keep of the castle was. A wall, I breathed deeply, walls then were made to walk on, if they were attached to castles, so that archers could stand on and defend them. Maybe, just maybe Anne had run out along that wall, hurting, in despair, wanting to die and had not thrown herself over but had collapsed in pain and anguish.

*   *   *   *   *

He was dead, my boy, my Edward. So full of life, how could it be? And I not there to comfort him in his last, pain filled hours.

I had seen the rider approach as I sat sewing with my ladies, gazing idly out over the lovely Vale of Nottingham. Seen the lone rider and thought nothing of it, until I heard one word - "NO!" - which seemed to echo and re-bound from wall to wall round and round the castle until it reached us, sitting in the Solar, enjoying the sun, warm through the glass and that cry, as loud as if to crack the glass and the walls too if it could.

"Richard!" - I don't remember leaving the room or how I got to the hall but I knew as soon as I saw his face and saw Hugh kneeling there. Faithful Hugh, who would leave my son for only one reason - and there was only one reason that Hugh would not be needed, would not be at our son's side, to teach and guide and protect. I said but one word - my son's name - not a question but an exclamation - for I needed no words, Hugh's presence told the tale, my son was dead, or he would not be here.

We ordered an Alabaster catafalque - designed by Richard - he modelled it on the one we had built for our second born son, George, named after his uncle and his brother George had named his youngest son Richard, after his own uncle. Both boys had died, as too had Edward's son, George. Both George's had lived three years - how hard it had been to lose my second son, and oh how hard to now lose the first.

Numb with grief I remember little of the next two weeks; dreading the time when we would have to leave, have to return to Middleham, not to visit our boy but to bury him. After the initial grief came the question why. Why had we not been there, why had I not been there and why did he have to die?

Hugh Burgh

How did a happy, healthy boy suddenly lose his life? All we knew was the physicians had done their best and that, in the end all they could do was ease his pain. No time to send for us, his parents - night had fallen and daybreak saw his last breath. Our only comfort being that Hugh was there 'til the last and his nurses, Ann, Jane and Isabel, Hugh's wife.

It was just over the year since the death of his namesake, Edward the King and Easter, falling a week later this year saw the death of my Edward. By the 26 April all was in readiness and the time to leave was at hand. Our final journey to our Middleham - once so dear - would hold only bitter memories for us now.

We stopped at York, as we always did with the inevitable ceremonies and expressions of sympathy then on to Sherriff Hutton to inform his cousins and then Nappa Hall putting off the time to ride to Middleham. As we approached the castle the good people of Yorkshire marked our passing, they stood in their cottage doors, in the fields, in the streets, taking off their hats and bowing their heads in silence, as we passed. They did the sign of the cross, blessing us and our dear, dead, son. It was May time again, another May, another year but this event was more devastating than that of last year, which had heralded Bishops Stillington's confession. Now I would think of May not as a beginning but as an end.

We travelled by slow stages, putting off the time that we would arrive in Middleham and so we arrived on 6 May.

His body lay in state - dressed and embalmed and ready - he was in his investiture clothes - his cap of maintenance with its tassel of gold - his mantle and train over him. We buried him the next day, at Gervaulx, walking in solemn procession behind his bier - all had been made ready by Hugh and the household - the last service that they could do for him, their prince. We had a private chapel there, behind the high altar and chapel where the monks prayed and held their services. Edward had many times gone and made offerings to the abbey - this was his household's desmesnes - fit for a prince and familiar to the boy and near enough to home, to Middleham. We had decided not to bury him at York or Westminster, yet it had to be somewhere fitting to his status as prince and familiar to the son and child.

The monks were waiting - lined up along the nave as, en-route, the villagers had been. Blessed at the high altar they carried him then out of the abbey church and round the back to our private chapel, his catafalque was there, waiting for him. I kissed his forehead for the last time and crumpled to my knees as I had on first hearing the news, felled by my grief, my ladies helped me to a pew, whilst he was interred. I think my heart broke as they pulled the cover over him, with his alabaster figure lying on the top. His cap and gown and all the accoutrements and shields painted, to show his rank and lineage and a carving of Richard imploring God and the angels to look after his son, our son.

He came towards me, after it was over - lifting me into his arms - both of us dry eyed, we had already shed so many tears up to this day. He led me out and the day was bright and I wondered 'how could it be - did they not know that the light had gone from our lives?' Then there was Hugh and Frances with horses for us to ride home, back to Middleham.

Richard finished giving the orders for the dispersal of the household and the disposal of his clothes - we both knew that we could not bear to return.

Our home now was in London, The Tower Palace, or Westminster, Baynards, Sheen or Windsor, Pontefract, or Richmond but never again Middleham.

We left early the next morning, I in a litter and Richard on horseback. My grief had taken me to the edge and I could not go back. I felt weak and ill and as I coughed there were flecks of blood on my kerchief.

*   *   *   *   *

What else could I do but hold them? They arrived, at last, to view their son's body and to bury him. All was ready as Richard had ordered, Hugh had come to see that his last offices to his young lord and prince were carried out as his lord and King had ordered.

So Edward was dressed in the clothes that he had worn for his inauguration as Prince of Wales, his coat hung long and his cap of maintenance on his head, he was laid out in the Great Hall for the people to view his body. Hugh stayed by the bier, dressed in deepest black, he would have stayed day and night to watch over his charge but Isobel had ordered him to rest and sleep and to eat something. Though I don't think any of us did much of any of this in those last weeks. All the boys had got on so well, age not seeming to matter, and now two were gone. I know he would go and walk around the rooms, remembering George and Edward and his own times with them, I caught him staring across the battlements towards the old castle where he would often find George and Edward playing.

I offered what succour I could but I was an old woman, how could I understand their boys' talk, their games, their hopes and dreams?

Their horses clattered into the courtyard, having left Nappa Hall at first light. We were expecting them and both Hugh and I had had the watch over Edward's body that night, to be there when they arrived. So we hurried into the courtyard in time for Hugh to help Anne from her horse. Emotionally exhausted, she almost fell into his outstretched arms. I hurried forward to take her into mine and Hugh turned to help Richard who was sat as white and still as marble; his eyes looking slowly round at the once dear, familiarity of Middleham. He too looked emotionally drained but he refused Hugh's steadying hand and dismounted.

"Is all ready?" he asked.

"Ay, my lord, as you wished," was Hugh's reply. He came to us then, my daughter and myself and putting his arms round us both said, "Come." Hugh also accompanied us into the hall and stayed by the door with me whilst they approached their son's bier.

He lay on Richard's white boar flag, my son, which covered one of the long tables in the great hall. It was cold; the fires had been allowed to go out to help preserve his body and even if the sun struck the building no warmth permeated into the rooms. Fires were usually kept banked low and turfed all summer for the nights were cold even when the days were hot, and a few hot embers could soon be raked and made into a roaring fire. But now the fires were out, the hall cold. He had died at Easter, on the 16 April and Hugh had got to us, at Nottingham in two days. I never questioned how but I expect that he used the relay horses that Richard kept stabled across the country, so that messages could reach him quickly. It was a system that he and Ned had devised, when Ned first became King. A week later we left Nottingham to begin a ten- day journey home. I don't remember much - only that Hugh was sent to make all the arrangements and that Richard designed an alabaster catafalque with an effigy of Edward on the top and round the sides shields showing his estate and Richard and I as weepers, Richard on one side appealing to God for mercy to his son and I on the other, appealing to Our Lady who carried the Lord in her arms. On the side also were the Neville arms quartered with the Plantagenet lions and the York falcon and fetterlock and the arms of England and Wales. At his head his own arms of Salisbury and those of Yorkshire at his feet. I stood and looked at him, my hope for the future, my companion at times as well as my son. Dead now and cold as the alabaster which would soon encase him, he looked a prince indeed.

As I watched, she seemed to freeze for a while, motionless until at last she extended her hand and touched his face, so gently and leaning over kissed his mouth. "Farewell, my son." She spoke softly. I had moved towards her when I saw her stop so still, afraid she would collapse but she smiled wanly as she saw my worried face. Her hand stretched out to me - "mother," it was an appeal. I went to her and she came into my arms, holding so tightly. I looked at Richard, he was the other side of the bier - looking at his son - drained of colour - his lips thinned and turned white. Hugh was by him, ready, in case he was needed but Richard nodded and turned and we followed him up to the solar.

*   *   *   *   *

My lady was asleep at last, in her mother's bed. My lord, ay and my King, had finished the last of his duties in his office. Suddenly he threw down pen and paper and jumping up strode out of the room. I hesitated momentarily then followed. He was nowhere in sight but I guessed his intent and made my way down the stairs to the great hall. Richard was their kneeling by his son, sobs wracking his body which shook with grief.

Chapter 12
Bosworth

I parked at Sutton Cheney lock to walk Pepi dog along the banks of the canal and up to the Heritage Centre. The walk was quite flat, across some fields and through a wood, some cows found us interesting and I put her back on her lead. I could see some activity going on and medieval tents had been erected, this was a bonus, a re-enactment group were camped on the field, by the centre and so I had a wander round, talking to people and watching them make things.

Inevitably we talked about Richard, why had he made that last, fateful charge. One man was definite, "he was like Jesus - he knew he was going to die. Why let Stanley leave Nottingham? He knew he'd be betrayed, like Jesus"

Was, that's what I believe, "Richard was no fool - he knew Northumberland would not support him. He knew he was going to die. I think he set it up - after all he had nothing left to live for - my God - he'd just lost his wife!"

*　　　　*　　　　*　　　　*　　　　*

Anne

I knew it was consumption - my sister Isobel had died of it in her 28th year. Child bearing and miscarriages and an emotional frailty we both seemed to have.

We would be unable to breath, sometimes, without difficulty, especially if it went suddenly cooler or very hot. At Middleham, when we were girls we seemed healthy enough - only mother forbade us to go out in the cold frosty morning air. She always insisted that we wait for the winter sun's warmth to permeate through the clouds, before we ventured forth from the cosiness of the solar.

*　　　　*　　　　*　　　　*　　　　*

Father could have left us in England - on his mad, treacherous, exodus to France. Edward would not have harmed us - no matter what, neither Edward nor Richard would take vengeance on women or children. We had been dragged from our beds - Isobel almost dropping her first child, into the stormy night and across an even stormier sea, to Calais. Father promised, "We'll land at

Calais. Wenlock will not turn his back on his friend Warwick and if he needed an excuse, well Isobel was about to give birth, what else in the name of a true Christian, could he do? We could take stock, in comfort and go on to France once the babe was born and Isobel stronger." This was the plan; father's will and he would make it so.

Only this time, this time it did not happen - this time it all went badly wrong.

At Calais Lord Wenlock refused to let us land - with regrets, and wine to ease Isobel's pain - and the riding and the cold and the storm swept seas took their toll of us all and the life of Isobel's son. With only mother and I - wide eyed and scared, unable to comprehend why we had been thus disrupted from our sleep — our warmth - our safety. Why, suddenly, my father was cursing York and praising Lancaster, swearing they would pull Edward's crown from his head and his seat off the throne.

My father had put him there and by God my father swore - he would topple Edward to a lower station than that to which he - Warwick - the kingmaker - had raised him. This boy, this upstart, this Earl of March, who dared to call himself Edward IV; with no Warwick to hold his throne for him, would be trampled back into the mire!

We would go to Louis, his friend, seek reconciliation with Margaret, Henry's wife and the Prince of Wales, Edward, and Henry VI would be returned to his rightful place, the throne of England.

Now mother and I, though we had been unable to save Isobel's son, fought for her life.

*   *   *   *   *

The first coughs did not worry me. I had been distraught - my son was dead. Our lack of children had not seemed to matter when we were at Middleham and Richard was Lord of the North. Taken to the hearts of the people in a way that was unprecedented, seeing he was not a Neville or a Percy - but he was just and when it was seen that the lowest would get the same justice as the highest, well then trust crept into the hardest Yorkshire heart and then love.

If only Edward, the King, had lived. If only Bishop Stillington had held his counsel. If only we could have stayed at Middleham. If only Richard had not been Richard - but then I'd not have loved him. Once he knew he had to act - he was a soldier, not a diplomat - he had kept away from the court and so did not know its ways, its intrigues and relied on friends to guide him, friends who had court experience, friends who put ambition first, friends who betrayed, friends whose only loyalty was to themselves.

Now his son, my son, our son was dead, suddenly and in excruciating pain and we had not been with him and I, I lost my will to live. What use was I to Richard, a barren Queen? Unable to produce another child, leave alone a son, a healthy son and heir. My grief and my guilt turned inward - and the coughs began.

I ignored it at first, 'twas only a summer cold, 'twould go as quickly as it had come', only it didn't; and Richard's frown of worry increased each time he looked at me. Despite his own loss, his own worries and cares, he was protective and caring as ever. Holding me through the night as I lay breathing with difficulty - taking deep breaths and feeling as if no air was in my body and I could not escape to Middleham anymore.

I coughed and coughed and then saw the flecks of blood on my kerchief. I decided I would have to take my courage into both hands and talk to our Doctor.

The Doctor did not pretend or try and give me false hope and all I could see before me was pain, suffering and death.

We sat by the fire that night, in our room. We held one another - Richard had spoken to the Doctor who had recommended that we sleep apart. Richard could not risk being infected because of me - we agreed, this would be our last night together - but that Richard would come to me every evening to see me and hold me and read or talk.

*   *   *   *   *

It was over. My lady was gone. She had left me forever. I knew it. It was inevitable from the day she first coughed and her kerchief was specked with blood.

Even as Queen she had kept out of the public eye. Gentle, good, loving, laughing, later to be termed frail. Her only frailty was her ability to love deeply - which meant a deep wounding, when those she loved, hurt.

All had known of her emotional pain when the Prince of Wales - her Edward - was taken from her, so unexpectedly, so suddenly, and none knew why. He had been born and grew up at Middleham - he loved the finer arts, enjoyed dancing but took after his maternal grandfather in his enjoyment of sport, especially falconry.

He enjoyed learning the art of war and was adept at drawing the longbow and he walked the moors with his dogs. In Middleham he was safe, even when my lady became queen he did not need a horde of servants to guard him. John, his half brother had gone everywhere with him, after Johnny died, and his guardian was Hugh - the King's body squire, most beloved and trusted, so naturally he was entrusted by the King to guard his son.

I, who had run my lady's household and helped organise the nursery, went with her when she travelled; either to London, or with the King. So I too was at Nottingham when the news, the dreadful news came, and Hugh had brought it, he blamed himself - but who can guard against death if he comes for you? How could stomach pains become so severe, so painful, that the doctor's could do nothing?

They gave him poppy juice to ease the pain and had stood about his bed, bewildered and frightened, what retribution would the King bring to them if they failed his son?

Thank God I was with her, for she had sore need of me, they had tried to give her something which would allow her to sleep but she threw it across the room, wringing her hands before dropping to the floor, crumpled with her arms across her body as if to hold her heart in - as it broke into pieces inside her and we who loved her could do nothing. My lord the King had been as bad as she - punching the walls he had screamed one word in despair, "NO!" I think the whole castle heard - certainly we did - sewing by the evening sunlight and talking low - a peaceful scene - until the echoes of that one word permeated and its ripples washed over us.

My lady's face drained of colour, "Richard," she whispered and was up - flying down the passageways to the hall where he had been meeting with councillors and friends - to determine the business of the realm - and I - all I could do was follow. Pages must have opened doors but we were unaware. My lady only aware of her beloved's pain - in that one word - seeking to comfort him and be his strength, as she always was - and I following - anxious. We had heard hoof beats and guessed a messenger but this would be on the King's business and nought to do with us - but that one word - seeming to echo round the castle altered everything - something was amiss and my lady went to him. He was stood on the dais in front of his chair, looking appealingly at the man at his feet - as if begging him to say the news was not true.

I remember my thoughts - wondering what had befallen - had Henry Tewder landed unexpectedly? It was then - as I drew closer with my lady, that I saw who knelt in front of the King, my lady also saw and sudden realisation of what news he must bring came to us - for only one reason would cause Hugh to leave the Prince's side - he who had been entrusted with Edward's care.

Richard came down from the dais - his arms outstretched - his reserve gone - his emotions raw - his desire to protect his queen, his beloved but from this there was no protection, no escape. She knew - as she recognised Hugh at my lord's feet - in deepest black - she knew - as did I. Her step faltered and she went into her husband's arms - she spoke only one word - a question to which she already knew the answer, "Edward?" He nodded, unable to speak and Hugh knelt all this time his misery plain for all to see. My lord waved us all away as he gently, so gently, led my lady away from our eyes and into the privacy of their own apartments.

I knelt before Hugh - and saw the pain and self-reproach, "tell me," and he did, faltering - with tears filling his eyes. "You did all you could," I told him, "none could have done more, and death cannot be defeated by Kings or Princes." I thought of how the late King, Edward, had died before his 41st birthday - and he so robust and strong - who would have thought it? "Even in life, we are in death," I quoted, it was no comfort but what else could I say?

A squire came, we were summoned, I to attend my lady and Hugh to tell his lord the details of his son's death. He would grieve but he was still King, with a duty to his people.

I got to her chamber but she was gone. Frantic I asked if anyone had seen her - which way did she go? The garden, was the reply, she said she needed air and wished to be alone. Leave her - they advised me- she will be sore wrath with you if you go to her now - she has given instructions - we are to let her be alone.

'Leave her!' Oh yes, I thought 'and if she comes to harm, what then?' churned with my own grief and anxiety for my lady I went into the garden. I knew where I'd be - there was not much room for a garden at Nottingham, it was on two high hills - with a moat - the view was extensive but she was used to Middleham and being able to walk or ride across the moors. So she had asked for a garden, with arbours and bowers covered in roses and honeysuckle, and heathers and wild flowers. A walkway was stepped - cut into the hill - for her and my lord - with a low wall and a rail - for it was easier to walk down, than up.

Here we had all sat many a day, talking and laughing, some reading, some doing embroidery and sometimes just the two of us, at ease in one another's company, not needing to speak. We would lean over the wall surrounded by trees and flowers and have a few idle moments before duty called us back.

She hung over the wall - her head dress gone and her hair tumbling down her back - a rich deep brown, with auburn lights and quite fair where the sun had caught it - I knew her intent and flung my arms round her waist and stroked her hair and whispered - "my lady," and then, "Anne." She turned at that, her eyes big and dark with bruising - showing her internal pain - she looked as if she had been punched. "My lady, come with me," and she let me lead her back - we got as far as the bower and she went in and sat down - looking lost and broken. I sat beside her and held her whilst she wept - my lady, my queen, but also my dear friend and cousin, whom I loved like a sister, I could do nothing but be there.

She, herself, was gone, with the King left alone to mourn her passing - for what was our sorrow, compared to his?

His doctor's had warned him not to share her bed - but by then she slept poorly and he was King and needs must sleep in order to rule, but he had never slept well in a bed if she were not beside him and I vow that after he left her at night to return to his own chamber to sleep, he spent many a restless hour.

Her ladies attended her day and night, taking it in turns to sleep on the truckle bed for as the end came nigh, we none of us liked to leave her. This day the windows were open, for March was, as always, changeable and this day - her last on earth - was bright and sunny - an eclipse was due and we had propped her up on pillows to see this phenomena. The King had come to watch it with her - her head on his breast, in the crook of his arm, which supported her. He was gently kissing her head and telling her how much he loved her. It took ages for the moon's shadow to fall over the face of the sun - we all stood at different windows to watch, all the people were out in the streets - it was a wonder, in our own lifetime.

I heard them murmur and her voice low - "look Richard," and then a few seconds of complete darkness - eerie but amazing. She had seemed to rally slightly - but as the moon blocked out the sun's light and then light once more returned - as we watched God's miracle so my lady, held tightly in her husband's arms, departed from us. Death had come and been kind to take her in so easy a fashion and the King lay with her still holding her - kissing her head and saying farewell - before - he sent for a priest to give her the last rites.

Now all he could do was to organise her a most magnificent funeral and he walked behind her hearse, bare headed - in deepest black - and so she was buried, in Westminster Abbey as was her right - at the doorway to the Confessor's tomb - with all London on the streets to watch and mourn. The folk brought flowers and threw them onto the street leading to the Abbey, for the horses to trample beneath their feet. She had been a gentle Queen and good - she had treated her nieces with love and respect - even sharing her Christmas gift, from the King, with Bess, the eldest. It had been a bolt of cloth of gold with gold tissue, from which they both had had dresses made. So, we knew, Elizabeth had done for her daughter when she was Queen, so my lady thought to show the world the high esteem in which her niece was held.

We walked behind the King, we ladies and the men of her household and with us walked Bess and Cecily, six paces behind the King, it was the last thing we could do for her, the last service we could perform. All cried, openly, and her lord and husband stood, as they lowered her coffin into the ground - tears pouring down his face.

Chapter 13
It is Finished

"He won't come out!" Francis stood in front of me, his hands wringing in despair. "He has locked himself in the royal apartment and will open to no one. Not to eat, or drink, we must do something."

He was appealing to me, this lord who was my lord's dearest friend and was lost, as we all were, without the King's strong hand. Now scurrilous stories were being told by Tewder's men that the King 'had killed his wife to marry his niece, Elizabeth.' He was locked in grief for his lady and had shut the door on the world and would let none in, and none but Francis had dared to try.

"I will go to my lord," I offered, "and see if, for old times sake, he will listen to me." The relief was evident on Francis' face. "Yes," he replied, "you go Hugh, try and get him to see that he must come out, he must rule or all will be lost."

So I went to him in their royal apartments. I who had fought by his side and carried the news of his son's death to him. Would he even listen to me? I sent the guard's away. "My lord," I called softly at first, then louder. "My lord Richard," no sound came, "'tis I, Hugh," still no sound. I would need to be cruel to be kind. "You needs must come out my lord, you must say it be not true." I paused and took a deep breath and my courage into my heart and spoke the words none else had dared say to him. "Tewder's spies are impugning the memory of the Queen, my lord, they do say that you had her poisoned." I waited and heard footsteps, the bolts were drawn back and the key turned in the lock. I don't know what I expected but I was met by a cold white fury in his face and steel in his eyes.

Chapter 14
Sisters

Politically it was a sound move and the Tewder knew it. He must have been scared and Morton, no doubt, had advised him to make the accusations publicly for maximum effect. They knew off his oath, to his brother's wife, knew he would not break it and marry his niece off against her wishes. So the rumour was spread, that the King himself would take his niece to wife.

She, poor lass, was caught in the storm, with her mother urging the match, the Wydville woman's only thought, to see her daughter as queen. No thought of Elizabeth's feelings or her son Richard's come to that. So Bess had been persuaded, by her mother, to write to Norfolk, who was close to the King and a respected elder statesman. 'If he would carry their cause to the King, Richard may well be persuaded' but of course the Wydville woman still did not know, or understand, my son. Even if consanguinity were not the bar Richard had loved Anne to the exclusion of all others. Given time he may well marry again and secure the succession but not now and certainly not his brother's child.

"Do they not see," he ranted at me, "that to allow Elizabeth on the throne I would be reversing the order of bastardy and therefore 'twould be young Richard who would be King now his brother is dead. Is the Wydville woman completely mad - or would she ignore her son's rights just to get one of her offspring on to England's throne!"

It became obvious from then that neither Elizabeth nor Cecily would be safe at court and so they were both sent to join their brother and sisters and cousins at Sherriff Hutton. Elizabeth confided in me, she did not fully understand, she loved Richard; he was her 'good uncle'. She had loved Anne, knew of her fears for Richard once she was gone and she, Bess, would prefer her uncle to the Tewder, her face screwed up and her mouth spat his name as if to get rid of a bad taste. Surely the Pope would allow a dispensation and it would make all secure again.

Richard was gentle with her - "and your brother?" was all he said and then she knew it could not be. That Richard did not want, as yet, her or any marriage if it was not Anne. He would not force any marriage on to her or her sisters to spite the Tewder's plans. He would fight, if it came to it and beat their enemy and he would keep England safe for all of them.

Reluctantly I accompanied the girls - young women now I mentally corrected myself - to Sherriff Hutton. After Middleham it had been Anne's favourite home. She had loved the gentle walks, the arbours and the water features, the work of generations of Neville's including my own mamma. It had become the official residence of my son George's boy, now Earl of Warwick, he was learning under Lincoln's gentle tutelage and his cousin, Edward had been part of the running of the household until he tragically died. So young George had become more confident, as Anne had predicted, so long ago it seemed but 'twas in fact a mere eighteen months. So much had happened, I allowed myself a sigh and I had wanted to stay near Richard at this most difficult time. His priority however was the safety of both his brother's children. He would entrust the girls to no one else's care but mine until they reached Sherriff Hutton safely. Myself and Tyrrell - who had proved so good and trustworthy a friend, who had brought Anne Beauchamp from sanctuary at Beaulieu; when Anne had borne her first son; to Middleham. Now she lived at Raby and had not been back to London, either for Anne and Richard's coronation or for her daughter's funeral.

The funeral had been worthy of Anne the Queen and Anne the mother, wife and friend. We had walked with all her household to Westminster Abbey, following the cortege that bore her through London's stark streets so that the people could mourn. Everywhere had been draped in black and the people stood silently, all bare headed and bowed. Only Queen for 21 months, yet she was loved by the common folk.

I sighed again, first Edward and then Anne, no wonder my son had walked the whole way with tears pouring silently down his face. Tears he refused to brush away as he had Francis' arm, which had been offered to him as they walked behind her coffin.

It had taken all Hugh's blunt talking to bring him out from behind his locked and bolted door, to deal with the rumours and false reports put about by Tewder's spies. A rhyme had been put up at Paul's Cross but a local man had it down in a trice, he had been seen to screw it up and throw it down and so, as these things sometimes do, it had come to Richard's notice. "Words cannot hurt me," was all he said. Francis however would investigate and found the network of Tewder spies.

Here, at Sherriff Hutton, it all seems so far away. I will visit Raby now the young people are all- together and tell Anne about the last two years of her daughter's life. I have a keepsake for her that Richard had taken from around Anne's neck, the Agnus Dei that was, at Anne's request, to go to her mother.

There was also a miniature of Anne, set in diamonds, which Richard thought she might like. 'Did he not wish to keep it?' I had asked and was told that he had portraits enough and what use were they? He had no need of a likeness to remember his love. I had noticed though that he took the Book of Hours, that she had given him, everywhere.

Now he was raising troops and preparing to meet the Tewder in open fight. Once the field was won things could get back to normal. I fingered my rosary and sent a silent prayer to heaven.

Chapter 15
The Road to Redemore Plain

It was a blustery day, not raining thankfully but chilly, despite it being April and the showers were kept at bay by the wind. This was a special day for me, not only my mother's birthday, God rest her soul, but it was my first public 'talk' about Richard III. He drove me there and supported me but the talk was mine, to be given to a party of American students, their teachers and the tour guide.

I had decided to make the stance of my talk from the view that nearly all actions taken by those who rule us, whether King, Queen and courtiers or Parliament all are part of a political game and the goal is very often not good governance but what can be gained. In this I felt that Richard III had been different, he wanted change for the good of the common weal, as well as the rich and as always, change can be frightening.

We had coffee and some lunch and then we were out in the courtyard of the Visitor's Centre. I was shaking as much from nerves as from the cold; the time had arrived, my chance to put my view of the events that had led to defeat instead of victory and to the onslaught of the albeit brief, Tudor dynasty.

*   *   *   *   *

Their were men milling everywhere, with billhooks and spears, longbows and cross bows, helms and chain mail and thick leather jerkins to protect against thrust and pike. It seemed a melee but order came quickly to the hillside, under cover of darkness the troops had been moved to the next high point from Sutton Cheyney, taking the prospective battle away from the village and overlooking Redemore Plain and the Sence brook, which regularly flooded it.

The King had prayed that night, or rather in the early hours of the morning in St. James' the little local parish church. In full armour he had knelt and received the host and asked God's blessing on the day's enterprise. Then we had been ordered, under cover of night, to set up camp and the King's standard on Ann Beam Hill, to put fear into Henry Tewder's heart when he woke, to see our army arraigned above him.

So here we were, in battle order suddenly murmuring and restless as the dawn broke, the King in his battle armour catching the first glint of the sun's rays, riding with his knights, to full effect, from the village to encampment; ready and waiting for him. The Duke of Norfolk, well seasoned in battle, and the King's friend, was at his side, with Northumberland charged with keeping the reserves in the rear. A short conference and the leaders took position with their men, the Tewder and his lot still hurriedly buckling on their armour and grabbing pike and bill hook, surprised by the appearance, out of the rising sum, of our army accoutred and ready to do battle.

Our allies, the Stanley brothers, could be seen by their banners, which flew proudly from Redemore plain and Sutton field, Tewder would be trapped between us; and the marshy area would not help his cause.

But no one is invulnerable in battle and de Vere, Earl of Oxford came at us up through the marsh and woodland and suddenly we were engaged in fearsome fighting. His company were on their own, we were sure to win, were winning - when like Chinese whispers we heard through the ranks that 'they have killed him, boys' ay - John Howard, Duke of Norfolk lay dead by his banner. It was a blow - who would lead us now? There was no thought of retreat but we had to have a leader. Then, there he was, the King himself, armour gleaming in the strengthening sunlight; so we could all see him; his circle on his helm, as brave as any, crying 'A Norfolk, a Norfolk,' he rode into our midst and lay about him with his battleaxe and we rallied to his cry; and his knights too now joined in the battle and his Lord of Oxford's troops gave ground before us, dying on the hillside or as they ran back through the marsh to the Tewder lines. We did not give chase - hold hard - we had been told and the King's knights re-enforced the order - 'hold the hill and you hold the day, don't be tempted to break ranks and chase the traitors and mayhap be trapped yourselves.' So we took a breather and watched the King, whose scouts were approaching with details of Tewder's movements, at regular intervals.

Tewder had begun to move his men round the hill to come up at us from the right, the Tewder banner flew proudly but he was no battle seasoned warrior and suddenly he seemed to be taking flight. Galloping across Redemore plain towards and round the hill he seemed to be heading towards the encampment of William Stanley, our ally.

Suddenly all changed and the next we knew was the King, followed by his 800 or so knights, was thundering past us, out of the protection of the trees and the marsh. We guessed his intent, to crush Tewder between himself and Stanley's troops, with my lord Thomas Stanley behind him he had no need to call on Northumberland to bring up the reserves, the King and Stanley's forces were sure to win the day and we set up the glad cry 'A Stanley, a Stanley' for we saw lord William's troops begin to advance towards the Tewder's galloping charger. We watched the scene from our vantage point, no need for us to join in now, our bit was done and we could watch victory for the King soon to be played out in front of us. William Stanley's troops appeared, nearer now, racing towards Tewder and the King, it was working, Tewder would be trapped between them and we shouted again, joining our voices with theirs, 'A Stanley, a Stanley'. Then it happened, we could not believe our eyes, the Stanley troops, our troops, or so we had thought, were fighting against the King and his knights, not with them. The tables had been turned by treachery and we stood and watched helplessly at first and then, gathering our courage we fairly ran down that hill to help our King.

Too late, for Tewder ran into the Stanley lines and they formed a shield round him to prevent the King, or any getting to him, the Stanley's had turned traitor to their lawfully anointed King.

Those of us who fought with him did not see the end, though we heard many tales of how our King was stabbed in the back, by the traitors. As the rout continued Stanley troops from left and right responded with wholesale slaughter and we heard that the Tewder ran to watch the ensuing carnage to a nearby hill, watching whilst his mercenaries and the Stanley's made sure that few left the field alive that day.

It is said that William Stanley found the King's helm and dislodging the coronet symbolically crowned the Tewder 'King of England'. Whilst the rightful King's body was stripped bare and hung, like a common criminal, over the back of a stray horse. He was taken to the monks at Greyfriars for all to see that the King was indeed dead. Yet when his Secretary, William Catesby entered the monastery to see his King's body, he was arrested for treason against the King! Tewder had declared himself King from the day before the fateful battle, so all of us who had fought for King Richard, lord and commoner, were deemed traitors by the Tewder monarch, and the magnates either changed coats, or died.

*   *   *   *   *

"That was really good," Rowena, said when I had finished, "only you don't need notes to read from, your own knowledge is good enough" I had done it and the students and teachers had seemed to enjoy the talk. I was shivering with nerves and the cold, "let's get the coats from the car," he said and the students presented me with a jumper from their College, which I gratefully put on. We got our coats and then joined them all as they walked the battlefield.

*　　　　*　　　　*　　　　*　　　　*

They were all dead, my brother, his eldest boy, my eldest boy and now Anne. We had gone to Middleham, she and I to see our son for the last time - ay and Middleham also - for we would not go back where once we had all been so happy. Sherriff Hutton was easier, our halfway house between Middleham and York it had many associations, not only memories of our son. Here I organised The Council of the North and here Edward had set up his household. I had also made it a safe place for my brother's children to live, until such time as they would find husbands and wives.

Now Anne, my most beloved lady, wife, friend, had left me, I was alone. It was put to me that I would needs must marry again, for the succession and for reasons of state, this I already knew of course, but Francis and Robert would have me think of marrying Elizabeth, Edward's daughter, to stop Henry of Lancaster boasting that he would wrest the throne from me and marry Elizabeth who would be his queen. It would be madness I knew, for she was still attainted bastard and if that were reversed 'twould be her brother Richard, who was entitled to the throne. Besides, I had promised their mother and themselves a free choice of husband and no fear of the Tewder upstart, who dared to call himself Richmond, would make me break my word.

I suppose I could have had her married off, to stop the Tewder boast but why should I? England was mine to rule and make safe and this I would do. Cecily had already fallen for one of my household, and, with her mother nothing loath, I agreed to their marriage. I would push nothing on to any of them for my convenience, this I had vowed and this I would keep, even though Elizabeth had written to me, saying that I was all to her and that she would do whatever I wished.

Anne was dead and they had got me to come out of my self imposed, solitary mourning. Hugh had come to tell me of the rumours that the Tewder spies were spreading around London. I sent Bess and Cecily to Sherriff Hutton therefore, so that no more lies or rumours could be spread and I made a public denial.

No, it probably was not necessary but the people of London had not seen me in many weeks, anything could be said and they would not know truth from rumour.

So I told them the truth and made my plans, visited my mother before she took the girls north and made my base at Nottingham to prepare for the Tewder upstart.

      *   *   *   *   *

Epilogue

Richard III's defeat at Redemore Plain - also known as Bosworth Field was political, it also transpires that a new form off fighting may have been used which we were unfamiliar with in England.

Edward IV had died in April 1483 and his son as heir apparent was waiting in the Tower Palace for his coronation, which was being organised. The everyday governing of the country was continued by the council which was left in place by Edward IV. Richard was Lord Protector but he lived first with his mother at Baynards and later, when Anne joined him, at Crosby Place and the new King held court at the Tower Palace, referred to by his father as his 'favourite palace'. The council and friends of his mother came and went freely to converse with the King and this was probably what led the Wydvilles to feel that they had a chance to 'try again' to get rid of the Lord Protector and to regain control of the King. The plot was uncovered by William Catesby, who though a clerk of William Hasting's obviously felt that a Wydville led Protectorship would lead to the similar troubles that had occurred during the minority of Henry VI, and even once he was King.

Once crowned Edward V would not come of age until he was at least 14 years maybe 16 years of age, he would rule with guidance and the Wydvilles wanted that guidance to come from them. They and the Lancastrians knew that with Richard of Gloucester, as Lord Protector their influence would not be great.

Richard had a council that was in place under his brother's Kingship and was not changed by him until the Hasting's plot was revealed and even then Morton and Thomas Stanley did not lose their positions.

The world was turned upside down when Bishop Stillington revealed that Edward IV had had a pre-contract, or betrothal agreement, given in his presence, to Eleanor Butler, who was daughter of the Earl of Shrewsbury (a usual practice in those days, a betrothal was a marriage, hence Anne was 'married' to Edward of Lancaster) and known as the Great Talbot, for all his victories in the wars against France. The acceptance of Richard as King and the ratification of his position by the Titulus Regius was received with a sigh of relief by all who realised that a boy King was likely to cause, once again, tussles if not actual battles, for the right to rule through him and no one wanted to go back to the days which later became known as the Wars of the Roses. During Henry VI's reign the Lancastrian nobles had milked the treasury and taken all the crown lands, so there was probably not a lot of faith in their ability to help Edward V rule fairly, and the Wydvilles had been seen as upstarts to whom the King had given money and positions due to their position of consanguinity to his Queen Elizabeth.

When Richard became King he saw a chance to put into practice for the whole of England the rules he had put in place as Lord of the North.

His first parliament was revolutionary and he abolished the practice of the King being able to demand 'benevolences' from his lords whenever he ran short of money, especially if preparing for war. If Richard borrowed money, history shows that he always repaid the debt. He realised that ultimately it was the peasants of the lord anyway who really paid.

Richard founded the College of Arms and Heraldry, which still exists to day, although Henry VII sent it 'underground', the college makes sure records are kept of all coats of arms and heraldry and thus prevents the use or mis-use of any person's coat of arms or livery, once these are decided upon and registered.

He initiated, with his brother Edward the first postal relay system, to enable letters and information to be sent to him and his brother, across the country, by horse, in a matter of days instead of weeks. He formed the Council of the North, which remained in place for over an hundred years.

King's college, Cambridge had been initiated by Henry VI and Edward IV gave to it generously to enable more building work. Richard too gave generously to King's and the Queen's college which his own Queen patronised, as had Elizabeth Wydville. They also visited and were very generous to Oxford University. The King always remembered his people of Middleham and Coverham and formed colleges for clerks and priests in both areas, this gave the ordinary people a chance to learn to read and write and to move into the clergy.

Edward IV was patron to Caxton who brought the printing press to London and Richard continued this patronage.

The magnates who had made their fortunes under Henry VI and had changed their allegiance to Edward IV began to realise that there was another change in the air. Ordinary people were now protected by the King's law and could no longer be thrown into gaol on a whim. They also had the right to appeal to the King in person, and were learning, as the dour northerners had, that the hearing they got would be fair, the lords and magnates thought that their power was waning.

When the dowager queen accepted Richard III as King she sent to her son, Thomas Grey the Marquis of Dorset to return home and to accept Richard, as King and Dorset would have returned had Tewder's men not prevented him. Was he a hostage? Who knows?

Henry Tewder took a gamble when he set sail for England. He had tried before and had narrowly missed capture, so he did not risk landing in England, which was loyal to Richard and landed instead in Wales. The people of Wales did not flock to his standard but they were, perhaps understandably, apathetic, why should they worry who was King it never improved their lot?

Tewder had nominal support from France and it was his last throw of the die, his men were mercenaries and ex-criminals and, new evidence seems to show that a crack troop of pikemen had joined him, introducing a way of fighting not encountered by the English up to this time. Richard had support from all over England and troops from the north were making their way to him when he decided to go into battle, and not to wait any longer. The battle of Redemore, later called Bosworth for the nearest market town, was lost mainly due to treason, from both the Stanley's, not well know for their trustworthiness.

Northumberland did not join in the fighting, was this because at the death of Harry 'Hotspur' in the reign of Henry IV the Percies had said that they would not lightly lose anymore of their sons to fighting for or against, the King? Certainly they never gave Edward IV much support, when he came to reclaim his throne in 1471. Maybe, in the reserve, he was too far away to be aware of what was happening. This did not save Percie's life when a few years later, whilst out collecting taxes for Henry VII he was pulled off his horse and murdered, for not going to 'good King Richard's aid' at Bosworth field.

The Stanley's seemed unable to decide who to back, Tewder was Thomas Stanley's step-son but this would not necessarily have mattered to Thomas, and it was his brother, William who changed history by deciding to protect Tewder from the furious charge which Richard led, when he hacked his way single handed through all Tewder's minders almost succeeding in his bid to confront Henry face to face, which he possibly would have done if William Stanley's men had not protected Henry Tewder.

It was an act of treason, for Richard was their anointed King to whom they had all sworn fealty. They were frightened that the changes Richard was making would take away their power and so they opted for Henry who they thought they could manipulate, as he was ignorant of Kingship or battle, they hoped he would rely on them and on their advice. They were in for a shock.

History was changed and it was also rewritten from this date, 22 August 1485 when as the York records show "Our lord, King Richard, late mercifully reigning among us, was most piteously slain and murdered, to the great heaviness of this city."

The Titulus Regius was banned and ordered to be destroyed; it is only through the braveness of Croyland Abbey who kept its copy, that this document ever came too light. The Tudor's had their historians write history in their own image and so men like Thomas More actually believed that Richard III, was a hunchback with a withered arm and leg, though how he was a battle commander, fought bravely, which even they had to admit, and leapt on and off horses, is a wonder if he was so disabled.

Thomas More did not complete his history of King Richard III, not because his boss Henry VIII had him murdered, as was previously thought, for he started writing it when quite young. Maybe this good and pious man was beginning to learn the truth? For it was not he but his son-in-law who had the work published.

The Shakespearean portrayal of Richard III as an evil, hunchback, conniving person, yet still able to win Anne Neville's heart, was as Paul Murray Kendall dryly observes, "a wonder for art but a disaster for history."

It is interesting to note that William Stanley was executed for treason against Henry Tewder, during the rebellion of Lambert Simnel, who pretended to be Edward Earl of Warwick, who was at the time confined to the Tower. The palace was beginning to gain its reputation for bloody deeds.

Anne Beam hill, now Ambion Hill was not in 1485 as it is now. The Victorians cut a railway through and there are now roads and fields that are not laid out as they would have been in medieval Britain. Many bones and cannon balls etc. have been found below Dadlington village and Bosworth has been known as Redemore plain and Bosworth Field. Most importantly Richard III now has a permanent memorial to his good lordship and Kingship, he was a King who the Tudor's tried to erase and then make into a monster and by doing so, through Shakespeare's parody of him, though only King for two years, he is perhaps the most talked about and well known Monarch in English history little is known about his wife and Queen, Anne Neville, like her husband Richard the Tudor version of who she was makes her seem weak and frail, but a woman who helped her husband run such vast estates and who became Queen at the same time as he became King, sharing his coronation to show their equality must have been quite a woman. No frail, weak creature she, as has since been thought. I hope that my portrayal of Anne may redress the balance somewhat and cause more people to question what we are given as 'history'.

*   *   *   *   *

Eboracum = Latin for York - hence the white rose symbolising York and the Boar where taken as Richard's badge, the white boar being his livery and maintenance badge.

End

www.ingramcontent.com/pod-product-compliance
Lightning Source LLC
Chambersburg PA
CBHW071219260626
47162CB00004B/1347